THE ROAD TO WAR

10-26-05 = 2+0

The Road To War

LEFT BEHIND®
>THE KIDS<

Jerry B. Jenkins

Tim LaHaye

WITH CHRIS FABRY

c. 2

TYNDALE KiDS

TYNDALE HOUSE PUBLISHERS, INC.
WHEATON, ILLINOIS

Visit Tyndale's exciting Web site at www.tyndale.com

Discover the latest Left Behind news at www.leftbehind.com

Published in association with the literary agency of Alive
Communications, Inc., 7680 Goddard Street, Suite 200, Colorado
Springs, CO 80920.

Scripture quotations are taken from the *Holy Bible,* New Living
Translation, copyright © 1996. Used by permission of Tyndale House
Publishers, Inc., Wheaton, Illinois 60189. All rights reserved.

Scripture quotations are taken from the New King James Version.
Copyright © 1979, 1980, 1982, 1991 by Thomas Nelson, Inc.
Used by permission. All rights reserved.

Characters in this novel sometimes speak words that are adapted
from various versions of the Bible, including the King James Version
and the New King James Version.

Edited by Lorie Popp

ISBN 0-8423-8349-2, mass paper

Printed in the United States of America

08   07   06   05   04
8   7   6   5   4   3   2   1

To Alex, Andrew, and Kevin Roberts

TABLE OF CONTENTS

THE YOUNG TRIBULATION FORCE

Original members—Vicki Byrne, Judd Thompson, Lionel Washington

Other members—Mark, Conrad, Darrion, Janie, Charlie, Shelly, Melinda

OTHER BELIEVERS

Chang Wong—Chinese teenager working in Petra

Tsion Ben-Judah—Jewish scholar who writes about prophecy

Colin and Becky Dial—Wisconsin couple

Sam Goldberg—Jewish teenager, Lionel's good friend

Mr. Mitchell Stein—Jewish friend of the Young Trib Force

Naomi Tiberius—computer whiz living in Petra

Chaim Rosenzweig—famous Israeli scientist

Zeke Zuckermandel—disguise specialist for the Tribulation Force

Marshall Jameson—leader of the Avery, Wisconsin, believers

UNBELIEVERS

Nicolae Carpathia—leader of the Global Community

Leon Fortunato—Carpathia's right-hand man

What's Gone On Before

JUDD Thompson Jr. and the rest of the Young Tribulation Force are living the adventure of a lifetime. After the GC corners Judd and his friends, darkness falls on New Babylon, causing many Carpathia followers to end their lives. Because of the plague, Judd and other believers can walk into government buildings and even concentration camps and help people escape.

Vicki and Lionel get a chance to fly to Petra and take it. Though it is difficult to say goodbye to their friends in Wisconsin, Vicki is excited about her new life and prays Judd will make it safely from New Babylon.

Judd returns to Petra, but the joyful reunion turns sad as live coverage of Chloe Williams' execution is shown on the Global Community News Network. Everyone is amazed at Chloe's brave attitude as she has one more chance to tell people the truth about God before she dies.

After linking up with their friends in Wisconsin by computer, Vicki and Judd are married in a small ceremony a few days later. Tsion Ben-Judah performs the wedding, and Lionel is Judd's best man.

Join the kids as they begin a new life together and try to survive the final days before the Battle of Armageddon.

ONE

Mysterious Message

LIONEL Washington smiled as he sat in front of a computer deep in a cave in Petra. He still couldn't believe that Judd and Vicki were married. He had been with them just after they had first met in Mount Prospect, and he would have never guessed they would wind up together. He replayed video from the ceremony a few days earlier and shook his head. *God worked this out,* he thought.

Chang Wong had set Lionel up with the computer and showed him how to access the Global Community's vast network. With a few clicks of the mouse, Lionel listened in on one of Nicolae Carpathia's secret meetings, or heard what was going on in the control room at the Global Community News Network. Chang had even given him software to control the computer with his voice, but Lionel preferred the old-fashioned way.

Lionel touched the stump of his left arm and counted the months since his accident in Indiana. He wasn't having nightmares as much, but he still found it hard to get to sleep. Sometimes he stayed up all night at the computer, trying to figure out what would happen next on God's timetable.

He had renewed his friendship with Sam Goldberg and Mr. Stein, eating manna and quail with them just about every day. But Lionel had to admit he longed for his friends back in the States. It was strange. He was in the safest place on earth, supernaturally protected by God from Carpathia and his growing armies, but Lionel longed for Wisconsin.

In a way, he felt useless and pitied. When assignments were handed out, Lionel was always given the soft jobs or nothing at all. He wanted to build things or help with chores, but he often found himself back at the computer alone.

As the yellow glow of the rising sun peeked through the opening to the cave, Lionel yawned and stretched. People would gather manna soon. Little kids would run through the camp. He loved playing with them, especially Kenny Williams, but Kenny spent most of his time with Buck now, asking questions about his mother.

Instead of heading for bed, Lionel clicked on the link for the Global Community in the United North American States. Things had gotten worse there in the past few days. The GC seemed to be taking out their frustration about the darkness in New Babylon on those without the mark. Reports of people being dragged from hiding places and executed had increased.

Lionel winced as he pulled up a report from GCNN detailing another raid on what looked like a militia hideout in Minnesota, fifty miles west of the Mississippi River. These people didn't have the mark of the believer or of Carpathia. They were hauled from their underground hiding place and herded onto trucks.

The camera focused on a smiling Commander Kruno Fulcire, head of the Rebel Apprehension Program. "We're very pleased with the level of cooperation from the people of this community," he said.

"How did you know they were here?" a reporter asked.

"We actually had a tip from family members of one of the unmarked. They, of course, will receive the full reward offered to those who help uncover rebels."

"Will there be more arrests and executions in this part of the country?" the reporter said.

Fulcire squinted. "I can't give that information, but we hope to have significant developments in the coming days."

Lionel sat forward and pulled up a map of the region. The site of the arrests wasn't that far from the Avery, Wisconsin, hideout. He quickly sent a warning message to Mark and the others.

Mark Eisman held his head in his hands while several people filed out of the main cabin in Wisconsin. Maggie Carlson put a hand on his shoulder before she left. Others weren't so kind, with mean looks and whispers.

Marshall Jameson paced in front of the computer. "I understand your feelings, Mark. I've wanted to start a rebel radio station to tell people the truth, but some things are too dangerous."

"Why are we so concerned about staying safe?" Mark said. "Isn't it more important to get the message out?"

Conrad Graham slapped his hands on his knees. "If that's your goal, I might go along with you, but you're talking about fighting

4

the GC. What could you possibly accomplish?"

"You saw what they did to Chloe," Mark said. "If somebody had tried to take those Peacekeepers out before they caught her, she wouldn't have lost her head."

"Reports from the Trib Force say she went outside trying to protect her family and friends," Marshall said. "But a rescue mission would have backfired. They didn't even know where she was."

Conrad stood. "I hate just sitting here as much as you do, but if you go out there, we'll be seeing your face flashed on TV."

"You guys don't need me," Mark said. "We have enough people to staff the Web site twenty-four hours a day with people left over."

"Okay, so what do you want to do?" Marshall said.

"Find those RAP people, Fulcire if I can, and give them a dose of their own medicine." Mark glanced at Conrad, then at Marshall. "If you want to know the truth, I've already packed my stuff."

Colin Dial sat in the corner. He cleared his throat and said, "What if we could find a way to get you closer to the action?" Marshall frowned but Colin held up a hand. "I don't want to see him get into trouble, but if he could get closer to the main headquarters, south of Chicago, maybe he could do some good before this is all over."

"What was the name of the lady and her son living near Chicago?" Marshall said. "The one Vicki and you guys met at the school-house."

"Lenore?" Conrad said.

"That's right!" Mark said. "She was staying southwest of Chicago, wasn't she?"

"I've got her number on my cell," Conrad said, handing a phone to Mark.

Mark punched the Redial button and waited. He heard a weird noise but no dial tone. "Something's wrong with it."

Mark found Lenore's e-mail address and looked through past messages to Vicki and the group. He quickly wrote her and sent the message.

Vicki awoke to sunshine peeking through the lone window of her and Judd's small dwelling. They couldn't call it a house, but it wasn't a shack either. There was enough room for a nice-sized bed, a cabinet to hold their clothes, a computer desk, and a small table.

Vicki noticed Judd was gone and smiled. There was no question where he was.

She lay back and stretched. Being married was a lot different than she had thought. There had already been disagreements to work through. Her childhood image of "happily ever after" was gone. Marriage was truly a lot of work.

Vicki thought of her friends in Wisconsin. They had seen the ceremony via computer, but it wasn't the same as being there. She would have liked Shelly and Melinda and Janie to be bridesmaids, but that had been out of the question. Life wasn't normal and never would be again. But within a few months Jesus would return. Vicki had lived the past six and a half years yearning for him to come back and set things right. Now she would experience the event with her husband.

Husband, Vicki thought. The word made her shoulders tremble.

There was a slight knock and Judd entered. "Ready for breakfast in bed?"

Vicki chuckled. "Are you going to do this every day until Jesus comes back?"

Judd smiled, set down a pitcher of cool water, and handed her a plate filled with fresh manna. "Wouldn't be a bad job," he said, sitting cross-legged on the bed. "You sleep okay?"

Vicki nodded. "Though it took a while last night. I kept thinking about lunch today. Have you heard anything from Dr. Ben-Judah?"

"I guess we'll hear something if it's off."

Vicki had figured she would get tired of eating the same food, but each morning the honey wafers tasted great. She recalled advertisements for restaurants that claimed their donuts or croissants melted in your mouth, but the manna literally dissolved on her tongue. It was light, flaky, and tasted good any time of the day. Vicki wondered if God had put extra vitamins in the food to satisfy their hunger.

"You know, we could have made a lot of money if we'd have gotten this recipe before the Tribulation started," Vicki said. "Even people who were overweight when they came here have lost pounds eating this."

"Just shows that God's food is best," Judd said, taking a bite of a wafer. He put the plate down and wiped his hands. "I know you might be tired of hearing this, but you've made me the happiest guy in Petra."

Vicki smiled. "I never get tired of hearing that. But sometimes . . ."

"What?"

"Well, I look at Buck Williams who lost Chloe and Dr. Ben-Judah who lost his wife and children. I see their pain and almost feel guilty for feeling . . . happy."

"I know what you mean. I met a guy yesterday who lost his brother and dad to the false messiah's vipers. Every day he wakes up knowing they're never coming back."

"I met a woman a few days ago who has family in Jerusalem. She doesn't think they've taken Carpathia's mark, but there's no way to tell. She can't reach them."

"Maybe we can bring this up with Dr. Ben-Judah," Judd said.

They finished breakfast, then took a long walk to the fountain. It was one of Vicki's favorite things to do—walk hand in hand with Judd around the sprawling camp, watching people, looking at the rock formations, meeting new friends. Vicki couldn't imagine being any happier.

Mark rolled his clothes and a small supply of food into his sleeping bag and tied it tightly. He slipped a gun Zeke had left behind into his pocket, but Mark knew there was no way he could overpower the GC. He would have to outsmart them rather than outgun them.

As he moved his things outside, he noticed Charlie standing by the window. The crisp, fall air was cool, and he could see Charlie's breath. "You want to come inside?"

Charlie nodded and entered, pulling his hooded sweatshirt over his head. He looked at the floor and blinked.

"What's up?" Mark said.

"I heard what you're thinking about doing," Charlie said, pawing at the floor with a foot.

"And?"

"And I wish you'd stay."

"Charlie—"

"But if you won't, I want to go with you."

Mark put a hand on Charlie's shoulder. "I'm sure I could use the help—but not this time."

"You know the GC are mean people, putting Chloe in that head chopper and all. They won't stop, and if they catch you . . . I think something bad's going to happen."

"Nothing's going to happen to me," Mark said. "I hope we'll all be together at the Glorious Appearing. I want to be standing right next to you when Jesus comes back."

Charlie looked up. "You really think we'll make it to then?"

"I'm planning on it."

Charlie helped carry Mark's things to one of the abandoned cars parked in the woods, then said good-bye.

Lionel stared at the computer screen, trying to figure out what he had found. An e-mail sent from an aide to Kruno Fulcire to the GC supreme commander updated the progress of the raids. Much of it was straightforward, with statistics about the number of prisoners and the execution schedule. But a line at the bottom included numbers and letters that looked like gibberish.

Chang walked in and Lionel stood. "Glad you're here. Take a look at this."

Chang sat and studied the screen. "Good catch. Have you talked to your friends in Avery?"

"I e-mailed them and even made a call, but I can't get through. I saw that GCNN was predicting some kind of satellite interference for the northern part of the States."

Chang shook his head. "No way. They must be jamming that area for some reason. When did you send your e-mail?"

"About forty minutes ago," Lionel said as Chang punched information into the computer.

"Look at this," Chang said. "The GC intercepted your message. It never got to your friends."

"What? How could they—?"

Chang clicked on the e-mail from Kruno Fulcire's aide. He pointed at the bottom of the screen. "See this? It's code for the higher-ups. I think they've finally broken into the Young Trib Force Web site."

"No," Lionel gasped.

"That's not the worst news. Looks like the GC has a location for your friends. If we don't alert them, they're dead."

TWO

Closing In

MARK shook hands with Marshall and hugged the others who had returned to the main cabin. Tanya Spivey thanked him for what he had done for her, her brother, and the rest of the group from the cave. Conrad patted Mark's back. Mark noticed Josey Fogarty wiping a tear away. He hugged little Ryan and patted his head, then moved outside.

Shelly was waiting. "We haven't always seen eye to eye on things," she said.

"I've been hardheaded. I'm sorry for the stuff I did that hurt you."

Shelly nodded. "This reminds me a little of when you went with the militia. Are you sure it's the right thing to do?"

Mark sighed. "I'm a militia of one now. No, I'm not sure this is right, but I just can't stay and wonder anymore." He glanced at the people coming out of the cabin and leaned close to Shelly. "You've been a good friend to me and the others. I've been talking with Conrad. He's a great guy. Give him another chance."

Shelly nodded and gave Mark a hug. Then he was off to the small car. The two-seater was perfect for him, fast enough to escape the GC in case he got in trouble but small enough to be able to hide in a pinch.

Mark checked his phone again and dialed Lenore's number. Nothing. She hadn't answered his e-mail, but he couldn't wait. He had general directions to her area, so he would try to get as close as he could before sunup and make contact then. He put on his night-vision goggles and kept the headlights off.

He glanced in the rearview mirror and saw his friends waving. Mark wondered when he would see them again.

Lionel hit the redial on his phone and got the same sound. Chang said the GC could jam certain cell or satellite phones, and it was possible they were moving in on the Wisconsin group.

Judd and Vicki rushed inside the cavern

with worried looks. "Naomi told us what's going on," Vicki said. "Have you gotten through?"

Lionel shook his head. "No phone, no Internet. And if the GC has control of the Web site, we can say good-bye to reaching out to people. They'll trash it as soon as they raid the hideout."

Chang hurried over and handed Lionel a printout. "I intercepted this from the United North American States. It was sent to the supreme commander about ten minutes ago."

Lionel scanned the paper. At the top was a string of letters and numbers. In the middle of the page was the message:

> *We continue to have great success rooting out rebels and would like to present the potentate with something spectacular today. We believe we have discovered a nest of Judah-ites hiding in rural Wisconsin. They have gone virtually undetected the past few months. We have also been able to tap into their Web site. We hope to have these rebels in custody by morning and turn the Web site into a tool for our cause. We will have them singing "Hail Carpathia" before the morning is out.*

Lionel slammed the paper on the table, picked up the phone, and dialed Wisconsin again. He still couldn't get through.

"What are we going to do?" Vicki said. "We have to warn them!"

"If I can reverse the jam on the phones we could call them," Chang said.

"Do it," Judd said.

Mark drove slowly down the narrow dirt road that led away from the campground. The road was little more than a path and had deep ruts from recent rains. The small car scraped bottom several times, and Mark was glad when he reached gravel.

A few minutes later he was on a paved road. He checked his map and headed west, hoping to hit a north/south route a few miles farther. Mark settled in behind the wheel and adjusted his goggles. In this part of the country he usually saw dead animals along the road, but there were none. He did notice the barren countryside, burned-up trees, and scorched shrubs. Looking through the goggles, a stream running through the hills looked like a long, green scar.

A light flickered on the horizon to Mark's right, and he slowed. It disappeared. *Was that my imagination?* he thought. To make sure, he put the car in neutral and coasted to a stop. He watched for any movement on the horizon but saw nothing.

As he pulled back onto the road, the light flickered again, and a line of vehicles rounded the hillside. He quickly gunned the car toward the stream and looked for a place to hide. His tires spun in the soggy ground, but he managed to keep going until he reached some rocks.

As the vehicles rumbled nearer, Mark got out and scampered toward the road. He was glad he had worn dark clothing, and he hunkered down behind a tree to watch the convoy.

The line of Humvees stopped a hundred yards away. A sleek, black truck opened, and several people got out. Definitely GC. But what were they doing here? Mark was too far away to hear, so he crept forward, duckwalking and trying to stay quiet. His goggles let him zoom in on the people, and Mark gasped when he recognized Commander Kruno Fulcire.

". . . heat imaging showed they were in this area, but we need specifics," Fulcire said into a radio.

There was a pause, and then a man on the

radio broke in. "We'll have those for you in just a moment, Commander."

Mark's heart raced. *Specifics for what? Had the GC finally discovered their hideout?*

He had to think quickly. There was no way he could start the car and race the GC back to his friends. They were sure to hear him and follow. Unless . . .

The radio crackled with a report from the satellite operator, and Mark returned to his car. He had driven several miles from the camp, but he guessed it was only a two- or three-mile trip through the forest.

Mark grabbed the phone and dialed Marshall.

Nothing.

Mark looked around the car's interior. He had ammunition, enough to keep the GC busy for a few minutes, but his main job now was to warn his friends.

He noticed the plastic gas can behind the passenger seat. Marshall had placed one in each of their vehicles in case they had to make a quick getaway and ran out of gas. Mark glanced at Fulcire and crew. He had to act fast.

Judd followed Vicki and Naomi through a maze of computers and workers. Since the beginning of the setup in Petra, Naomi had grown in influence as a first-rate computer operator, then as a teacher. She was the daughter of one of the elders at Petra, Eleazar Tiberius. She not only had technical knowledge, but she also helped teach workers how to answer spiritual questions on Tsion's Web site, which was read by as many as a billion people every day. There were now thousands of computers and counselors spread out through the camp.

"How did Dr. Ben-Judah hear about the situation?" Vicki asked, struggling to keep pace with Naomi.

"I talked with my father, and he mentioned it to the rabbi," Naomi said. "He asked me to get you and move your meeting up from lunch."

Tsion smiled and welcomed them to his tiny living room. "Please, sit. Is there further news?"

"Chang and Lionel are working on getting in touch with our friends," Judd said.

"It's so hard when we're this far away and can't do anything," Vicki added.

Tsion clenched his teeth. "We felt the same way with Chloe. I have a feeling we are going to be doing more mourning in the days to come. Oh—" He put up a hand—"I did not mean that your friends will be harmed, but evil is rising. Antichrist and his followers are desperate."

"We understand," Judd said. "It's just that we know angels warn people. Is there any reason why God couldn't do something like that now?"

"God's ways are God's ways. I do not presume to understand why he chooses to keep some from the blade while others are taken from us. I do not understand why he chose me to lead a million people here, but I am grateful he made me part of his plan. I do not think there is any harm in asking him to act—in fact, I think he wants us to. So let us pray now that he will use some angel or human to save your friends and keep them safe."

Mark rushed to the stream and up a hill to a grove of charred trees. Behind him the vehicles pulled out and continued. "Come on," he whispered.

He had reached a knoll when a terrific blast shattered the night. Flames shot into the air, then another explosion. Mark had stuffed a rag in the gasoline can, lit it, and placed it under his car's gas tank.

The lead truck in the convoy stopped, and

several troops jumped out, weapons ready.
An officer shouted something, and the last
vehicle turned sideways on the road. Mark
didn't wait to see what would happen. He
scrambled over the knoll, got his bearings,
and headed for the camp.

He kept dialing the phone as he ran but
couldn't get through. Depending on how long
the GC remained occupied by the burning car,
Mark had a chance of getting to his friends.

Vicki felt better just hearing Tsion's voice. His
prayer showed a deep reverence for God, yet
she could tell how much God was his friend.
When Judd prayed, Vicki felt the emotion.
There was something about talking with God
together that touched her.

When they had finished, Tsion asked about
their home and how their marriage was going.

Judd said they were getting along fine and
asked if Tsion had any advice about what to
do when they disagreed on certain issues.

"I hope you do disagree," Dr. Ben-Judah
said. "You have two different perspectives. But
the beauty of a relationship built on God's
love is that he has brought you together to
make you one. This does not mean that you
won't fight about certain things, but if you did

not have conflict, you would never have the opportunity to grow and learn and change. I suspect you will mature as believers more in these last six months than you have the last six years."

"Did you have fights with your wife?" Vicki said.

Tsion laughed. "We had pouting sessions at first. I would get hurt and pout for a few days. Then she would get hurt and pout for a week. She was much better at pouting than I was, let me tell you. But as we grew together, and especially after we became believers in Jesus, I saw our relationship change." He sat back and closed his eyes. "Oh, how I long to speak with her and ask her advice on things. But then I won't have to wait long for that, will I?"

"You mean when Jesus comes back to set up his kingdom, right?" Vicki said.

"Yes. I am confident that I will see my wife again and that we will have quite a reunion, along with my two children. How I long for those who have not yet believed in the message to do so. As you know, there are some who have come into Petra lately who are not believers, and I want them to hear, but I also want people outside to believe a new message God has been impressing on me."

"Why don't you put it on the Web site?" Judd said.

Tsion nodded. "That is one idea I have considered, but I would like to reach even more people, those who haven't stumbled across my teaching on the Internet. I believe God has given me a message he wants even Nicolae and his followers to hear."

"Chang seems to be able to do a lot with the setup here," Vicki said. "Can't you break into international television?"

Tsion scratched his chin. "Hmm. Chang is quite resourceful. I will need to talk with the elders and Captain Steele, but that is an excellent idea."

Judd talked about the fact that he and Vicki almost felt guilty for being so happy when people were mourning.

Tsion smiled. "Joy and sorrow go hand in hand. Do not feel guilty for the good gift God has given. Enjoy each other and praise God with your love."

Judd brought up Vicki's idea about starting an orphanage after Christ's return. "In one of your messages you mentioned there could be many children who go into the kingdom who don't have parents."

"Yes, I believe that will be true," Tsion said.

Vicki blushed when Judd elbowed her. "Well, I was watching a news report about the Junior GC program the other day. There are so many young kids who've been brainwashed by Carpathia. They will need a lot of help, and I was thinking we could—Judd and I—find a place where we could take some kids in and care for them."

"The need will be so great," Tsion said. "I am thankful you are thinking ahead to such a time. The truth is, these children will probably have about a hundred years to decide."

"A hundred years?" Vicki said.

"Ask Naomi to print out the section of my teaching that deals with this. I think you will find it quite helpful."

Before they left, Tsion led them again in prayer for their friends. Vicki thought of little Ryan and the others in Wisconsin and prayed that they would be kept safe.

THREE

Mark's Run

MARK ran through the forest and realized he didn't recognize anything. He heard the faint crackling of fire behind him and guessed the convoy was still inspecting the explosion. Mark needed to find something familiar—like the road. If he didn't, the GC could locate his friends before he did.

Mark turned to his right. The goggles bounced on his face as he jogged, so he took them off. Without them, he could barely see. He finally put them back on and slowed, making sure he didn't trip over dead branches or dips in the ground.

A thousand thoughts flashed through his mind. His friends had no idea of the danger. He imagined the GC breaking into each cabin and hauling people out. Charlie would be so scared. Mark knew Tom Fogarty kept a gun in his cabin, but what good would it do?

Mark picked up his pace, the night-vision goggles bouncing crazily. It had been a long time since the group had even thought about a GC raid. When they had first arrived, Marshall had conducted surprise drills, but that had been so long ago Mark doubted anyone would remember what to do.

His legs ached from the pounding. He wanted to stop and rest but knew he had to keep going, keep moving toward his friends. He was their only chance of survival.

If he stopped, they died. Simple as that.

Mark felt a rage that pushed him on. He hated Nicolae Carpathia and everything the Global Community stood for. The man had brought such death and destruction to the world, and people still followed him. Mark recalled a different version of "Hail Carpathia" that Judd had sung:

> *Hey, Carpathia, you're not the risen king;*
> *Hey, Carpathia, you don't rule anything.*
> *We'll worship God until we die*
> *And fight against you, Nicolae.*
> *Hey, Carpathia, you're not the risen king.*

Mark chanted the words softly as he ran, moving his feet to the words. He had never been much of a singer, and his cousin John had made fun of him in church once. Mark smiled at the memory. John had been killed at sea by a giant wave, and Mark had never really gotten over John's death. Sure, he had gone on with his life and tried to help others come to know God, but John was always in the back of his mind. What would have happened if he had stayed with the group, instead of heading east and getting drafted by the GC?

There were so many what-ifs in Mark's world. The biggest was what would have happened if he had believed the message *before* the Rapture. He wouldn't have seen all the destruction, plagues, and deaths of friends.

His heart beat wildly and he gasped for air. He searched his mind for some verse of Scripture or words from a song to keep him going, but nothing came.

"God, I don't know why this is happening, and maybe you wanted me to go out tonight because you knew the GC were coming," Mark prayed. "But whatever the reason, you put me here. Now help me reach my friends before it's too late."

Lionel clicked on the computer's world-time function and saw it was 3 A.M. in Wisconsin. If the GC carried out their plans, they would catch his friends in the middle of a Bible study, trying to get the Web site running again, or worse, sleeping.

Lionel had never seen anyone work as hard as Chang at trying to override systems, but finally Chang threw up his hands. "I'm sorry, Lionel."

A report from Commander Fulcire had sparked a bit of hope. "Explosion nearby—may be an attack," the report said. But a few minutes later another report dashed Lionel's hopes. "False alarm. Explosion linked to dead Judah-ite's car. Someone may know we're coming, which means we're on the right track. Proceeding to target."

"It's in God's hands now," Chang said.

Lionel shook his head. "I wish there was something more we could do."

Chang put a hand on Lionel's shoulder. "When I was in New Babylon, many times I felt like there was nothing I could do. But I realized the greatest thing any of us can do is pray and ask God to work out his will. You see, God really is *for* us. He wants to help us through difficulties. I used to think he should just take us out of them or solve them for us. But sometimes I think he shows himself greater by walking through our troubles with us. So let's invite him to have his perfect way in your friends' lives and in our lives too."

Lionel nodded, then bowed his head. He prayed first for Mark.

A verse finally came to Mark, but it wasn't the one he wanted to think of. *"The greatest love is shown when people lay down their lives for their friends."*

Mark didn't want to lay down his life, though he had seen that done many times in the past six years. He thought of Natalie Bishop who had worked for the GC, Pete Davidson who had led the GC away from the kids, and Chloe Williams.

Mark had watched Chloe's execution with a mix of fascination and horror. The appearance of the angel at the event had raised many questions. Had he spoken with Chloe? Was that where she got the strength to be so bold at the end? And why didn't the angel rescue Chloe and the other believers who were executed?

Mark's right leg stuck in a hole, and he felt a sharp pain behind his knee. He stumbled forward, then fell back, grabbing his leg and screaming. He pulled his foot from the hole and rolled to his left side, holding his leg and rocking.

When he tried to stand he fell. He couldn't

imagine taking another step, let alone running the rest of the way.

Something rumbled and the convoy approached. Mark lifted his head and realized he was sitting next to the dirt road leading to the cabins. The ground vibrated as the first Humvee approached, and Mark held his breath. "Keep going," he whispered, putting his head back and closing his eyes.

Mark expected to hear brakes squeal, but the vehicles roared past. *They missed the entrance!* Mark thought. *Maybe they're not after us.*

When the last Humvee passed, Mark struggled to stand. He managed to put his weight on his left leg, but his right felt like a knife was sticking through it. He hopped up to the road and nearly passed out from the pain.

With short steps and hops he started toward the cabins, finding that putting his hand behind his right knee helped. He took off his belt and buckled it around his leg. The pressure seemed to work.

He kept going as quickly as possible. When he reached the trees surrounding the cabins, he left the dirt road and yelled for his friends.

Mark heard a noise to his right—something running. He set the night-vision goggles to macro and saw two eyes rushing for him.

Then he heard it. The most wonderful sound in the world!

Phoenix's bark!

"Come here, boy," Mark said, sitting on the ground and gathering the dog in. "Go on back now and make some noise."

He patted Phoenix's back and sent the barking dog away. Mark limped farther and saw a light in the distance from the main cabin. The door opened and someone called Phoenix.

"Help!" Mark hollered.

"Mark?" It was Marshall. "What are you doing?"

"Please, we don't have much time! Come get me."

Marshall and Conrad carried him to the main cabin.

"GC, they passed me on the road. They're coming here."

"How do you know?" Conrad said.

"I don't have time to convince you. Just get everybody out of here."

Conrad nodded and hurried outside.

Marshall sat Mark on a chair and inspected his leg. "You might have torn some ligaments. We're going to need to look at it—"

"We can look at it later," Mark said. "Do we have enough vehicles?"

"We should. What happened to the car you took?"

Mark told him.

Marshall scratched his chin. "We have the 15-passenger, another minivan, and some smaller—"

"Get them ready," Mark said.

Tom Fogarty rushed inside. "I have Josey and Ryan in the van. Everybody else is gathering."

Marshall handed him the keys. "Start it up while I help Mark to the—"

"No," Mark interrupted. "I'm going alone."

"That's crazy!" Marshall said.

"Go! I'm going to torch this place."

"What if it's a false alarm?" Tom said.

"It's not," Mark said. "It might already be too late. Now if you value your wife and son, go."

Tom rushed outside.

"When you get to the main road, go west," Mark said. "And keep your lights off. I'll follow as soon as I'm finished."

Marshall hesitated and Mark pushed him toward the door. "Call Petra. Once you get far enough away from here, a cell might open up. Chang might be able to block the satellites they're using to find us."

"We'll head for Lenore's place," Marshall said. "We'll meet you there." He gave Mark keys to a different car and hurried into the night.

Mark watched Charlie turn and wave. Janie and Shelly smiled at him.

When they finally pulled out, Mark grabbed lighter fluid and poured it on their computers. Anything that might lead the GC to someone inside the Tribulation Force or Young Tribulation Force had to be destroyed. He lit a match in the main cabin, took a deep breath, and threw it on the fluid. With a loud *whomp*, the fire began.

Mark hopped to the next cabin, tossing lighter fluid and a lit match inside. He knew this would attract the GC, but it had to be done.

Each step was painful, but Mark managed to make it to the end of the row of cabins, lighting fires and getting away. He hobbled back past the main cabin as the fire whistled and cracked. Mark found his car, a diesel, and it chugged to life. He pulled out, the fire lighting up the forest behind him. He pulled onto the path and gunned the engine.

He came to a stop at the main road and pounded his fist on the steering wheel. "Take that, Fulcire!" he whooped.

Mark turned the wheel to the right and started to pull out but stopped. He couldn't leave now. The GC would come back and see the fire, then go after his friends. Maybe there was something more he could do.

He turned around and headed back into the trees. He would figure out some way to delay the GC. Anything for his friends.

Four

Commander Fulcire

LIONEL prayed for those in Wisconsin as Chang clicked his way through the Global Community network.

When Chang got through to GC satellite operations, he gasped. "They've got images of the hideout in Wisconsin!"

The screen showed a wide shot and a glow coming from the ground. Chang zoomed closer. "There's a fire."

Lionel's heart sank. "We're too late."

"Maybe not. I know the GC likes to burn people out, but if they knew this was Young Tribulation Force headquarters, they wouldn't have burned it before they got all the evidence." Chang clicked on another computer and turned. "The latest message from Fulcire is a request for location, not a report that they've caught the rebels."

Lionel glanced at the satellite image. "So you're saying our people might have figured it out and torched the place?"

"It's possible," Chang said. "And if so, they're on the run. Which means we need to lock this thing up so the GC can't track them."

"You can do that?"

Chang smiled. "We can do lots of things." His fingers flashed over the keyboard like lightning as he went deep inside the satellite operation. "They won't even know what hit them."

Five minutes later, Chang clicked his mouse a final time and sat back. "Want to know what they're seeing right now?"

Lionel nodded.

Chang clicked on the satellite image and crossed his arms. A huge, yellow smiley face appeared. Underneath was written, *Temporarily out of service. Thanks for your patience.*

"Awesome," Lionel said.

"Now let's listen in on the satellite control room," Chang said. He clicked a few more keys and brought up audio of people shouting and cursing.

A female worker tried to figure out what had gone wrong. "I don't understand it, sir. One minute I had a bead on these rebels, and then the image was gone."

"Sir, Commander Fulcire is calling!" someone yelled.

The man cleared his throat and punched the speakerphone.

"This is great," Lionel said.

"Commander, we're having some technical difficulties, but my technician said she's tracking your convoy and you've gone past the location. It should be easy for you to locate now. There's a fully engaged fire there."

"We're heading back that way and can see the flames. Can you give me exact coordinates?"

The man replied with a list of numbers Lionel didn't understand. "But with this fire, there's a chance the rebels are on the run."

"Do a heat imaging of the area to see if you can locate any vehicles or people getting away."

"We can't, sir. As I said, we're having some technical difficulties."

"Do you know how long we've been working on this?" Fulcire shouted. "Don't give me technical difficulties. I want answers or heads are going to roll!"

"Yes, sir, we're working on it, sir," the man said. He hollered at the others, trying to motivate them to fix the problem. Everyone seemed angry at the yellow smiley face.

Chang clicked the keyboard again and smiled. "I can't wait to hear what they'll say when they see this."

The smiley face changed to a frowning face. Underneath it were the words, *We're so sorry you're having trouble. Keep a positive attitude and maybe you won't lose your heads.*

Lionel thanked God for David Hassid, who had originally designed this computer center. While Chang worked his magic, trying to keep his friends safe, others answered questions from believers and nonbelievers around the world. It was estimated that a billion people every day got information from Tsion Ben-Judah's Web site, and the many mentors around Chang and Lionel were hard at work with Tsion's cyberaudience twenty-four hours a day.

"Let's just hope this buys our people enough time to get out of there," Chang said.

Mark parked the car behind some trees away from the cabins and stumbled to a hiding place. His knee throbbed. The lower part of his leg tingled since the belt had cut off his blood circulation. He sat on the ground, his back to a tree, and tried to stretch his leg, but it only brought more pain.

The fire and smoke glowed against the black sky. Ashes rose overhead, and trees near the cabins caught fire. Branches and needles crackled.

Mark heard a rumbling and noticed the convoy on the main road. Instead of taking the dirt road, which Mark was sure they couldn't see, the convoy went down an embankment and cut across an open field. They finally found the dirt road and drove through the trees to within fifty yards of the burning cabins.

Mark crawled closer to the vehicles while GC officers jumped out to inspect the cabins. The lead vehicle, a smaller black truck, parked closest to the main cabin, and a tall man got out, cursing.

Fulcire, Mark thought.

"Check every cabin and the perimeter behind them," Fulcire shouted. "I want these rebels now!"

As the officers ran, Mark got an idea. Everyone was so intent on following orders that no one paid attention to the vehicles.

He pulled himself up and staggered to the last Humvee. After making sure no one was inside, he quietly opened the driver's door. His heart beat like a freight train when a light went on and a *ding, ding, ding* sounded. He quickly found a button on the doorframe and pressed it, turning off the light and the sound.

Mark grabbed the keys dangling from the ignition, pulled them out, and stuck them in his pants pocket. *One down*, he thought.

Vicki sat on the bed reading the printout Naomi had given her, fascinated with the words of Dr. Ben-Judah. This section dealt with the one thousand year millennial kingdom of Jesus. She giggled.

Judd turned from his computer. "What's so funny?"

"I was just thinking about my life before the Rapture. I would never have dreamed I would be so excited about reading stuff about the Bible."

"All we've been through has a way of changing your mind about a lot of things," Judd said. "What's in there?"

"Tons. For example, Tsion believes that in the one thousand year kingdom, God's going to lift the effects of original sin."

"How?"

"Well, he says it's going to be a lot like the Garden of Eden. All the people who rebelled against God and the bad angels will be gone."

"And not on vacation." Judd smirked.

Vicki continued, "God's going to bind Satan so he can't tempt people, and Christ— with the help of angels and believers—will basically enforce God's laws. Everybody will have their own home. There won't be war—"

"That verse about turning swords into farm plows or something . . ."

"Yeah, Tsion includes that here. It's from Isaiah 2. 'The Lord will settle international disputes. All the nations will beat their swords into plowshares and their spears into pruning hooks. All wars will stop, and military training will come to an end.' "

"I can't imagine a world without war, can you?"

"We won't have to imagine it. It'll be reality soon."

"What else does he say?"

Vicki turned a page. "Here it is. According to Isaiah 65, Tsion says people will live as long as those before the days of Noah. That means a believer who is born near the beginning of the kingdom could live almost a thousand years."

"No way."

"Another verse says a person will still

be considered young at the age of one hundred."

"Sounds ideal."

"Just think about it," Vicki said, putting the pages down. "No more drug addicts. No more thieves and murderers. The stuff on TV won't be so violent. Everybody's going to know about God because Jesus will be the true King."

"I still can't get my mind around it," Judd said.

"The people who enter into the kingdom in their natural bodies, hopefully like you and me, will still be able to die. There's just so much to learn about—and think, we only have a few months until the whole thing starts."

"The best thing is, we're going to get to see our friends and family. You'll finally get to meet my mom and dad—and my little brother and sister."

"I can't wait," Vicki said.

Mark moved to the next Humvee, but this time he threw the keys as far as he could into the trees. As he crept toward the next vehicle, someone approached from the other side and Mark hit the dirt, the pain in his leg almost making him cry out.

"We're searching now, but my guess is they're not here." There was no question that this was Fulcire. "What's our intel on their movement?" After a pause, Fulcire cursed and yelled, "Can't you people do anything right!?"

Mark breathed a sigh of relief when the man walked toward the main cabin. The front window was open in the next Humvee so he quickly reached inside, snatched the keys, and tossed them into the woods. This time they pinged off a tree.

Fulcire turned. "People! People! I heard something in the woods to the east. Everybody over there—now!!!"

Mark stayed low to the ground, watching officers move away from the burning cabins. *Perfect,* he thought. *One more set of keys and I'm outta here.*

Mark sneaked to the lead vehicle and pulled himself alongside the driver's window. The tinted glass kept him from seeing inside. He carefully opened the door, and an alarm pierced the night.

"Somebody's messing with the vehicles!" a man shouted.

Mark reached for the keys, but they weren't in the ignition. He pulled the handgun from his pocket and shot out the left front and rear tires as he limped toward the last Humvee.

He pulled the keys from his pocket, opened the door, and struggled into the driver's seat. The Humvee roared to life while officers streamed from the woods.

Mark slammed the gearshift in reverse and backed away as the first volley of gunfire hit the Humvee. *Bulletproof glass*, Mark thought. *Lucky me.* In spite of the pain in his leg, he jammed his foot on the accelerator and rocketed down the dirt road, bullets clinking off metal, dust and rocks thrown in the air. In his side mirror he saw flashes of fire from the soldiers' weapons.

Mark focused on the road and turned on his lights. As he neared the main road, he glanced back and saw the frantic officers trying to find their keys. He smiled, knowing he was free.

But he wasn't.

As soon as he turned onto the main road, a bus careened in front of him, cutting him off. Mark jerked the wheel to the right, plunging into a ditch. The Humvee shook and rattled. A sharp pain shot through his right leg, and Mark nearly lost control. As the Humvee jumped out of the ditch, the driver of the bus swerved. Another ditch, this one deeper than the last, loomed in front of him. Mark struggled to keep the vehicle on the road, dodging to his left and hitting the bus, then lurching down the hill into dead trees. He slammed on his brakes with his left foot and watched the bus zip past. Peacekeepers ran forward, shooting at his tires.

Mark whipped the Humvee around and headed east. He was going sixty miles per hour when a Peacekeeper with a rifle opened fire, exploding a front tire. He lost control and veered left as a back tire shredded.

The Humvee, tires smoking now, ran off the road and slammed into a burned tree, knocking it down and sending Mark into the windshield.

Dazed, Mark shook his head and tried to see how badly he was hurt. He felt his forehead and pulled back a handful of blood. He felt like someone had hit him in the face with a baseball bat.

Gotta get out of here, he thought, reaching for the door handle.

The door opened by itself, or so it seemed. Mark swung his legs around and leaned into the barrels of several Global Community guns.

"We have him, Commander," one said into a radio. The man grabbed Mark's gun and threw it away. Then he twisted Mark's hands behind him and cuffed them.

Mark went limp and collapsed.

FIVE

In the Trap

MARK awoke in the back of the bus, hand-cuffed and aching. His right leg felt like it was hanging on by a thread. His belt was still buckled tightly around his knee. His eyes stung, and he realized blood had trickled down his forehead while he was unconscious. He leaned forward to the seat in front of him and rubbed his eyes for relief.

The Peacekeepers weren't happy. They had expected to fill the bus with rebels. A Humvee followed, and Mark figured Commander Fulcire was in it.

Mark sat back and tried to get comfortable. His shoulders throbbed, and his hands had fallen asleep. He tried to pray and remembered a verse Marshall Jameson had talked about during one of their meetings—the one about the Holy Spirit praying for believers

47

with groans that can't be expressed. At the time Mark hadn't understood the concept, but now he was living it. Though he couldn't form the words, God knew what was going on.

Mark had often thought about what he would do if he ever got caught by the GC. If he kept his mouth shut, he couldn't go wrong. The moment he talked, they would offer things—food, water, or sleep. But Mark was desperate to know if his friends had truly made it to safety. If he knew that, he could keep going as long as it took.

Mark knew of others who had been captured. Chloe Williams had no doubt been questioned by the GC, and while news reports said she had given lots of information, no one believed it. He shuddered at the thought of facing the guillotine. If he was going to die as bravely as Chloe, he knew he would have to have God's help.

I'm not going to die, Mark thought. *My friends are going to find me and get me out of here. Period.*

A Peacekeeper glanced at Mark. The soldier looked a couple of years older than him, and Mark wondered if he had heard that within six months Jesus would return to crush the Global Community. *He's coming back soon*, Mark thought. *Sooner than you think.*

The soldier sneered and keyed a micro-

phone attached to his uniform. "He's awake,
sir."

"Condition?" It sounded like Commander
Fulcire.

"Looks a little dazed," the soldier said.
"Still breathing."

"Give him some water. Nothing else."

The soldier unscrewed the cap from a
bottle of water and held it out. Mark opened
his mouth, and the man poured a few drops
in. Then he poured so fast that Mark choked,
coughing and sputtering.

The soldier laughed. "Get enough, Judah-
ite?"

Mark caught his breath.

The soldier sat across the aisle and leaned
close. "You ready for what they're going to
do to you? No mark, no head. But since you
caused trouble back there, I think they're
going to make it even more painful for you."

Mark wondered how the GC had found
out about their hideout. Had they tapped
into their phones? Or infiltrated the Web
site? Had someone tipped them off?

I guess it doesn't matter now, he thought.

Mark didn't want to talk, but he had to
know about his friends. "Seems like a lot of
people for just one guy." His throat felt
scratchy and raw.

The soldier smiled. "No way you were working alone. We've got the others in custody. They'll face the same fate as you." He leaned closer and whispered, "They say the blade sticks sometimes. It can cut you a few inches, and they have to raise it back up and let it go again. If you talk, they give you a clean one that gets it over quick."

Mark thought about Jesus—how he had endured mocking and torture. Before the soldier could say anything else, Mark slumped against the seat and fell asleep.

While Vicki read more of Tsion Ben-Judah's printout, Judd jogged to the tech center for an update. He spotted Rayford Steele, Chloe's father, and watched him walk toward the meeting place. Over the past few months, Rayford had reorganized the Tribulation Force. Mr. Whalum, who had flown Lionel and Judd to South Carolina, had taken over the Co-op and helped plan the movement of supplies throughout the world.

Rayford had agreed with a daring plan by Chang to bug an upcoming meeting in Baghdad, where Nicolae's ten kings were supposed to appear. Judd had asked Chang if he and Vicki could be part of the tech crew,

but Judd knew Rayford would have the final
say. Judd didn't know much about the plan,
just that Chang hoped to use hidden cameras
and microphones. There was even talk of
Zeke making special disguises for everyone.

As Judd entered the tech center, Lionel
waved frantically.

Judd rushed over and found Chang watching satellite video of a fire. Lionel explained
that it was the Wisconsin hideout, and Judd
gulped.

"Darrion just got through on the phone
and is going to call us back any minute,"
Lionel said.

"Did they all get out?" Judd said.

Lionel shrugged. "Let's hope so."

Chang went to the kids' Web site and
explained how the GC was able to break in
and discover where the Young Trib Force was
headquartered. Judd felt sick when he saw
Nicolae Carpathia's picture on their Web site.
The GC had not only removed any reference
to Jesus, the Bible, and Tsion Ben-Judah, they
had already posted several articles about the
great Nicolae.

*If you've been to this Web site before, you'll
notice a number of changes,* one post read. *We
have to admit we were wrong about the Global
Community and especially Potentate Carpathia.*

If you haven't taken the mark offered by the GC, do it now. It's painless and it'll help them keep order and peace. After all, that's what we all want.

The article was signed *Vicki B.*

"We worked so hard on that," Judd said. "All that data, all the articles . . . everything's gone?"

Chang frowned. "Unless you have originals, I'm afraid so."

The phone rang and Chang put the call on speakerphone. It was Darrion.

"Where are you guys?" Lionel said.

"Illinois. We finally got the cell phone working just across the Illinois border and got in touch with Lenore. She and the others in her group had to move, and we're heading there tonight."

"What's your location now?" Chang said.

"We found an old farmhouse that wasn't destroyed in the fire," Darrion said. "As long as the GC doesn't use their satellite stuff to find us, we're okay."

"I've taken care of that," Chang said.

"Did everyone get out?" Lionel said.

"Everybody but Mark. He stayed and we haven't heard from him."

Judd bit his lip. "How did you guys find out the GC were coming?"

"Mark limped into camp telling us we had

to get out. Marshall thinks he ran into the GC along the road."

"Where was he going?" Lionel said.

"There was a big fight and Mark decided to leave," Darrion said. "Everybody was upset with him, but I guess if he hadn't left, the GC might have found us."

Lionel asked about Charlie and several other members of the group. Darrion told them they had escaped with Phoenix, but all of their supplies, computer equipment, and clothes were still in the cabins.

"The cabins don't exist," Judd said. He told her about the fire.

"You guys settle in and stay safe," Chang said. "I'll jam their satellite until you make it to Lenore's."

Mark noticed the sun rising to his left. They were heading south toward Chicago. Maybe they were taking him to the new GC headquarters he had heard about. Or a prison where they televised executions.

Mark tried to put the thought out of his mind. He had memorized a lot of Scripture, so why couldn't he remember anything now?

As he sat in the rumbling bus, emotion overtook him. Tears dripped from his nose onto the seat. He tried holding them back, but that only made things worse. Sobs racked his chest, and he thought he would die.

"Please, God," he prayed, "give me the strength to go through whatever is going to happen. I know I won't be able to make it without you."

Vicki's heart raced when Judd told her what had happened to their friends and that the cabins had burned. The news about Mark sent a wave of panic through her.

They rushed to the tech center, where Chang was at a computer on the other side of the room working on jamming the satellite. Lionel was at another computer in the back and waved at them.

"Just got into the GC's database," Lionel said. Vicki was amazed at how fast Lionel could type one-handed, his fingers rushing back and forth among the keys. "Chang showed me how to see anything Fulcire sends to his superiors. We can't hear phone conversations, but we'll see any written info." He clicked on a previous message and something beeped. "New message."

This confirms phone conversation that there will be a press briefing this afternoon, Fulcire wrote. *We'll go over the raid in Minnesota and the capture of this new rebel. We do not have a name yet, but I assure you we will by the time of the briefing. Though he's young, we think we've caught one of the big fish in this so-called Young Tribulation Force.*

Vicki put a hand to her mouth and whispered, "Mark."

"I wish we could send out a message to have people pray," Judd said.

"We could do it on Tsion's Web site," Lionel said.

"Can you make that happen?" Judd said.

"Just tell me what you want it to say, and I'll have Chang post it."

Vicki gagged when she saw the kids' Web site. She thought of all the articles the kids had carefully created. Mark had rewritten most of Tsion Ben-Judah's messages especially for young readers. Now it was all gone

Vicki, Judd, and Lionel spent a few minutes praying for Mark and asking God to protect him. "Let Mark know that you love him and that you're there for him," Vicki prayed.

SIX

The Visitor

MARK scooted close to the side of the bus and propped his head against the wall. The emotion had passed, and now he just felt tired and sore. The cuffs cut into his wrists, and he wished the Peacekeeper would loosen them.

Mark tried to think of something to take his mind off the pain. His first thought was Vicki, and he smiled. She had looked so pretty on the video feed from Petra. Beautiful. He had known early that Vicki was attracted to Judd. Mark's own feelings hadn't stirred until much later. He loved the sound of her voice, the way she took chances to help people. There was something fearless about her, something pure and noble.

"You gotta forgive me, Vicki," Mark whispered. He felt bad about yelling at her at the

Dials' hideout in Wisconsin. He had told her she had to leave or he would, but the truth was, deep down, Mark was simply confused about his feelings. Now he knew he felt jealous of Judd and had lashed out at her in anger.

Later, when he and Vicki had talked, he had almost told her how he felt. Almost let her know that he wanted to be more than friends. Mark took a deep breath and tried to hold back the tears. It was okay that she didn't know, almost better.

The bus rumbled on as the sun rose higher. Peacekeepers slumped in their seats, trying to catch a few minutes of sleep. A man Mark hadn't seen before walked down the aisle. He wasn't wearing a GC uniform. The bus driver stared straight ahead, not noticing the man.

As the man neared, Mark looked closer at his long robe that reached the floor. He passed the Peacekeeper in the seat next to Mark, stopped, and looked directly into Mark's eyes.

"Who are you?" Mark croaked.

The man's eyes seemed full of compassion, as if at any moment he would weep. He gave a slight smile. "A messenger."

"Okay." Mark hesitated. "So what's the message?"

The man gathered his robe and sat. "Lean forward," he said. The pressure on Mark's shoulders suddenly relaxed. The handcuffs fell, and the man placed them on the seat.

Mark rubbed his wrists and put his head back. His neck muscles, which had been so tense, loosened. The feeling was heavenly. "I think I could sleep for a hundred years. How did you do that?"

The man smiled. "It's not important for you to know the how, just the why."

"All right, why?"

"Your heavenly Father knows your needs. He has heard the cry of your heart and has sent me."

Mark sat up. "Is this a rescue? Are you taking me out of here and past all these Peacekeepers?"

The man looked at the floor. "This is the message I was sent to give you. 'When you go through deep waters and great trouble, I will be with you. When you go through rivers of difficulty, you will not drown! When you walk through the fire of oppression, you will not be burned up; the flames will not consume you.' "

"Who are you talking to?" the bus driver said, looking in his mirror.

The man nudged Mark. "Don't worry. He can't see me. At least, not yet."

Mark ignored the driver and lowered his voice. "What does that verse mean? That you're not going to get me out of here?"

"The Father has not promised to snatch you away from trouble. But he has promised to be with you every step. You have served him well, Mark. You will serve him yet."

Mark moved his leg and noticed he had feeling below the knee. He quickly untied the belt and removed it. No pain. "Did you do that?"

The man put an arm around Mark's shoulder. "In Proverbs it says, 'An unreliable messenger stumbles into trouble, but a reliable messenger brings healing.' "

Mark flexed his leg. The torn ligaments were healed and without surgery—at least normal surgery. It was all he could do to sit still. "What do you mean, I'll serve him? I don't even know where these guys are taking me. How am I going to serve God from some GC jail?"

The angel—for Mark knew this was what he was—closed his eyes and spoke. It was like a whisper to Mark's heart. " 'Have you never heard or understood? Don't you know that the Lord is the everlasting God, the Creator of all the earth? He never grows faint or weary. No one can measure the depths of his understanding. He gives power to those who are tired and worn out; he offers strength to the weak. Even youths will become exhausted, and young men will give up. But those who wait on the Lord will find new strength. They will fly high on wings like eagles. They will run and not grow weary. They will walk and not faint.' "

Mark was overwhelmed by the words and felt a sense of hope. "I have to know if my friends are okay. Can you tell me?"

The angel stood. "Your actions and the actions of friends far away enabled them to escape. They are safe."

"Thank you."

The man turned. He was only inches away from a Peacekeeper, but the GC soldier kept sleeping.

Mark wondered if the angel had caused the others to sleep. "Do you have to go?"

"We will see each other again before the end." He leaned toward Mark and with a twinkle in his eye said, " 'The Lord is my strength, my shield from every danger. I trust in him with all my heart. He helps me, and my heart is filled with joy. I burst out in songs of thanksgiving.' "

The angel turned and walked toward the bus driver. Mark pulled himself up for one more glimpse, but the angel was gone.

The bus driver slammed on his brakes and shouted, "Hey, take care of your prisoner! He's gotten his handcuffs off!"

"How did you get out of those?" a Peace-keeper said, pouncing on Mark.

Mark just smiled and held out his hands. He remembered Vicki's favorite chorus that the group had sung at the first hideout in Wisconsin and began singing.

Laughing, crying, and singing to God. It was a song of joy and thanksgiving.

Lionel watched news reports from the United North American States alone. Using codes Chang had given him, he was able to tap into a live feed from an unnamed prison.

The female reporter began with footage of the night before when a camera crew had caught the action in Minnesota. As far as Lionel could tell, these were militia members and not believers, though the reporter labeled them "suspected Judah-ites."

"Another raid early this morning brought the arrest of a high-level member of what the Global Community called a rebel youth movement responsible for many deaths and destruction of Global Community property."

"We're looking forward to interrogating our prisoner," Commander Fulcire said with a wink.

"Why aren't you going to execute him for not taking the mark?" the reporter said.

"Normally we would, but we believe this prisoner has valuable information. What we have here is a troubled young man who has been brainwashed to believe our lord Carpathia is evil. I'm not making excuses for his crimes, but if we can go inside his head and get information about other members of this dangerous group, we'll be that much closer to the kind of world peace we've been striving for the last few years."

The camera cut to a shot of Mark being led off a bus, handcuffed and shackled at the ankles. He saw the camera and started to say something, but the Peacekeeper behind him hit him on the head with the butt of his rifle and Mark fell.

Lionel closed his eyes and gritted his teeth. The reporter parroted the GC's lies. *If they knew the truth about Mark and the others in the Young Trib Force . . .* He shook his head. *No, if they knew the truth, they'd still report lies because they're under the control of the biggest liar of them all.*

The woman concluded her report and

threw it back to the anchor at the Global Community News Network. Lionel kept watching the live feed, wondering if she would say anything once she was off the air.

"How did that come off?" the woman said. "Did you get a shot of the guy yelling about Jesus?"

"Yeah," someone said from behind the camera. "But we cut the audio out of his Jesus line. The producer didn't want anyone saying that name."

Though GC officials tried everything to get Mark to give his name and information, he kept silent. He didn't want to be traced to Nicolae High School and his friends in the Young Trib Force.

After they processed him, Mark spent hours waiting in an interrogation room. He finally got so tired that he put his head on the table and went to sleep.

His dreams the past few years had been filled with nightmares of GC raids and fires, huge, dragonlike creatures chasing him, and the one repeating dream of being caught by Nicolae himself. But this time he dreamed of golden streets filled with light, love, and laughter.

Mark awoke to a slamming door and looked at the clock. Had he really been asleep six hours, or had they changed the clock?

Commander Fulcire placed a plate of food on the table and sat. Chinese. One of Mark's favorites. He tried not to look hungry, but his stomach growled.

"I heard you wouldn't tell us your name," Fulcire said. He took a mouthful of fried rice, chomped into an egg roll, and wiped his mouth. "I know you think we're evil, but we can be quite nice to people who give information."

Mark was determined not to say anything that would hurt his friends, and he didn't want to talk at all, but he couldn't resist this chance. "My mom always taught me not to talk with my mouth full."

"She did? And what was your mother's name?"

Mark stared at him.

"Let me tell you something about this facility. There are isolated cells where you'd be alone, and there are general population cells where we put you with other . . . how should I say this? . . . criminals like yourself. These aren't nice people. They don't believe in much of anything other than their own survival. We put a nice young man like you in with them, and who knows what awful things could happen."

Mark sat back and thought of what the angel had said. God was going to use him in some way.

"Tell us your name or you'll go into one of those cells."

Mark stared straight ahead.

"Suit yourself," Fulcire said. He finished the meal, scraping every piece of rice from the plate, and walked out of the room.

When he was gone, Mark bent over and tried to lick some of the sauce from the plate, but that only fueled his hunger.

A round man in a green sweater walked in with another plate of food. He glanced through the window on the door, put the plate in front of Mark, and took Mark's handcuffs off.

"You need to hurry and eat that," the man said. "They could be here to get you any minute."

Mark grabbed a plastic fork and pushed some fried rice into his mouth. He was so hungry he almost inhaled the food. The man seemed fascinated with how quickly Mark could eat.

"Why are you helping me?" Mark said.

The man shook his head. "Can't stand the way they treat people. I don't care if you don't have Carpathia's mark, you're a human being." He held out a hand. Mark shook it and kept eating.

"Fulcire is a decent man. He just wants to know some information so we can process—"

"So he can process my neck with the blade," Mark said.

"We're getting information from the others who were staying with you."

Mark smiled. "You didn't catch anyone because there wasn't anyone to catch."

"I'm just trying to help. I don't want to see you suffer any more than you have to. If there's something you'd like to talk about, tell the guard you want to talk to me—"

The door opened and Fulcire barged in. "Cummings, what do you think you're doing?"

"I'm sorry, sir. I was just—"

Fulcire swatted the half-eaten plate of food from the table, and rice flew onto the walls and floor. "Get him out of here!"

A guard rushed in, seized Mark, and took him through a series of doors. Another guard released Mark's feet and pushed him toward a row of cells. The room stank, and Mark thought he would throw up at the smell. The guards took him to the largest cell where at least five people slept on cots pushed against the walls. They handed Mark an energy bar, shoved him inside, and slammed the door.

Two large men stood and approached him. One was bald, and Mark guessed he weighed three hundred pounds. The other was a smaller black man with a stubbly beard.

The bigger one pulled something sharp from his pocket and held it out. "Give me that food or we'll cut you!"

SEVEN

The Mission

JUDD and Vicki sat in their home, wondering what Mark was going through. They had seen the video report Lionel had recorded and read the messages Commander Fulcire had written. No doubt the GC was gloating about this new arrest.

Judd felt confident that Mark wouldn't tell the GC anything important, and even if he did, their friends were headed to safety. The two prayed for Mark again, asking God to help Mark be strong.

"Do you think they'll torture him?" Vicki said.

"They'll do anything to get information." Judd took Vicki's hand. "You know how this is going to end."

Vicki nodded and tears welled in her eyes. "I hate this. We all know it can happen after watching Chloe. I still remember the feelings I had when they caught Pete. You hope something miraculous happens, you pray that God will step in, but deep down you know your friend is as good as gone."

Judd sighed. "I can't imagine what Buck is going through after losing Chloe."

"I talked with Priscilla Sebastian earlier. She's watching Kenny when he's not with Buck or Rayford. She said Buck basically spends his waking hours taking care of Kenny or writing."

"Makes sense. Staying busy probably keeps him sane."

"I've volunteered to watch Kenny whenever they need a break."

"He really likes you," Judd said. "You'd make a good mom."

Vicki grinned. "I don't know. It seems like such a huge responsibility." She paused. "But if that's what God has for us, to be parents, I'm up for the challenge."

Judd touched her shoulder. "I've been thinking about all that time before the Rapture. My parents wanted me to become a godly man—I didn't even know what that meant, didn't care. I think I want the chance to pass God's love on to other people, kids. And maybe they're not ours. Maybe they're kids without parents like you're talking about."

Vicki smiled and hugged him. "Sometimes

I see my mom's face in my dreams. She loved me so much, and I didn't even know it."

"I remember catching my mom praying for me one night. I've never told anybody about it. I was coming home late from some party that I shouldn't have gone to, and I slipped in without anybody hearing me. I thought they'd all be asleep, but when I passed my parents' bedroom, I saw my mom in her reading chair, the light on behind her."

"What was she doing?" Vicki said.

"Crying. And she was whispering a prayer—I heard my name. I always felt bad that I didn't tell her I was home. I just went to my bedroom."

Vicki groaned. "It makes me so sad to think what I was like before all this. It's almost like I wasn't alive—I was just a shell looking for something to numb myself even more, so I drank or smoked or did stuff to help me not feel anything."

Judd nodded. "I guess if you don't have God, you don't want to feel anything because it's so scary. You're all alone."

"Yeah, and that's what makes being a believer so great. You can finally be alive. I think about the verse that says the evil one comes to steal and kill and destroy but Jesus came to give real life."

"That's what I want. Even though life can bring a lot of pain and can really be awful, I'll take living it with God's help rather than being a spiritual zombie."

Mark nervously handed the larger man his energy bar. "I'm not really that hungry."

The man tore it open, broke it in half, and gave some to the bearded man. They ate, then retreated to their bunks.

Mark looked for an empty cot but found none, so he went to the corner and sat on the floor.

A young man, Mark guessed he was in his thirties, slept nearby. The man opened his eyes. "What'd they get you for?"

Mark shrugged. "Guess I didn't want to cooperate with their rules."

The man lifted his head and stared at Mark. "Hey, you don't have Carpathia's tattoo."

"Don't like tattoos. Especially the GC kind."

The man smiled, showing missing teeth. "Same here. I dodged it for as long as I could, then got caught and thrown in here yesterday. Sure seemed like the GC was in a hurry with something big. I guess they'll make us take the thing or chop us sometime today."

"What did you do wrong?"

"Sure are nosy, kid," the bearded man said from across the room.

"Lay off him, LeRoy." He turned back to Mark. "I'm Steve. We were doing a little relocation of goods when the GC found us."

"Problem was, it was the GC's goods we were relocatin'," LeRoy said.

"What do you mean?" Mark said.

"We got caught taking some electronic equipment we wanted to sell," Steve said. "Some stuff out of a GC warehouse a few miles from here. That was LeRoy's idea that I said was too risky—"

"We'd have gotten away with it if you could have kept your big mouth shut," LeRoy said. "This is the last place I wanted to wind up."

"He was in before for murder," Steve said. "Got loose during the big earthquake. Been on the run since."

Mark looked at LeRoy, remembering Lionel's story about his uncle being killed by a man named LeRoy. "What's your last name?"

"Banks. What about it?"

That's it! This is the same guy! "Nothing," Mark said. "The name just sounded familiar."

"Well, you can forget it because I'm gettin' out of here and away from this deadwood of a partner you're talkin' to. He's going soft on me anyway, talking about that Ben-Judah guy."

Mark looked at Steve. "You've been reading Dr. Ben-Judah's Web site?"

Steve nodded. "Had a lady talk to me about God and tell me I should read it. I did, but I didn't understand it."

Mark glanced at the men in the next cell. "Are there others here who don't have Carpathia's mark?"

"I don't know. Ask 'em," Steve said.

Mark stared down the row of darkened cells. He had no idea how long he had before the GC came back for him. "Excuse me," he began nervously. "I don't mean to wake you, but how many of you—?"

"Shut up!"

"We're trying to sleep, stupid!"

Others cursed him and threw things at the cell bars.

Mark took a breath and kept going. "Just give me a minute and answer this. How many of you in here don't have the mark of Carpathia?"

"Shut your yap, jerk!"

Steve hurried over to Mark. "You'd better watch yourself. These guys'll turn on you fast."

"I don't know how much time I have left in here. I have an important message, and if I don't talk now they may never hear what I have to say."

"Your funeral," Steve said.

Mark continued. "If you haven't taken the mark of Carpathia, I want you to listen. You still have a chance to believe the truth."

A handful of men rolled from under their blankets and looked at him.

"What do you mean, the truth?" Steve said.

"I think some of you are ready for what I'm about to say. God's been working on you."

"I'm going to work on *you* if you don't shut up," someone said. "LeRoy, take care of this kid."

"Shut up and let him talk," LeRoy said. "I got a feeling he won't be here much longer."

Mark nodded at LeRoy and turned to face the men. "When the disappearances happened, did any of you lose friends or family members?"

"Of course we did," a man said. "Every-body did."

"Okay. Now think about those people. Were any of them religious? Did they talk a lot about God and go to church?"

"My mother-in-law vanished and it made me religious," a man said. "I thanked God for a whole year!"

The others laughed.

Mark studied the unmarked men. "The

reason those people vanished is because God came back for his true children. They were immediately taken to heaven, which is where they are today. That means every one of us in here didn't know God. Anybody who was left behind missed the truth."

He took a step to his right. "You might have gone to church or grown up hearing stories from the Bible. I know a lot of people who lived good lives but were left behind. The truth is, everyone still on earth never asked God to forgive them, and they never turned away from the bad stuff they'd done."

Mark lowered his voice and explained the prophecies about Antichrist and how each of the plagues the world had seen had been predicted thousands of years earlier. Then he spoke of the prophecies concerning the Jewish Messiah who would come not just to save Jewish people but all who believed in him.

"That man's name is Jesus," Mark said. "He was God in the flesh, and he lived a perfect life and died in your place on the cross."

"Why would God have to die to let us go to heaven?" a man said.

Mark paused, trying to think of a way to explain. "God is the great judge of every person, and because he's holy, he can't let anyone into heaven who's not perfect. Is there any one of you who's done everything right?"

"My wife always thought she was perfect," a man said, and the others laughed.

"Everybody falls short of God's standard," Mark said. "We're all guilty and deserve to be separated from him forever. But instead of punishing us, the judge *himself* became a prisoner, lived a perfect life, and then took our sentence."

"What's this got to do with us?" LeRoy said. "This ain't church."

Mark focused on the few men standing who had no mark. "God is offering each of you a key to unlock the cell that's holding you. That cell is sin. It traps us and keeps us from following God. In the end it will kill our souls if we don't ask to be forgiven."

Someone in the back moved and a cot creaked. That was the only sound Mark heard.

"What about those of us who took that mark?" a man said from a few cells away. "I didn't want to take it, but they made me."

Mark pursed his lips. "I don't know what to say. The Bible says anyone who takes the mark of Antichrist is condemned."

A clamor rose so loud that Mark thought the guards would come. He retreated to his corner and prayed for wisdom.

When things calmed, Steve tapped him on the shoulder. "Some of the guys want to know what to do. Will you tell us?"

Mark looked up and saw those without Carpathia's mark standing with their faces pressed against cell bars. A door opened down the hall, and Mark heard footsteps.

"Okay, listen carefully," Mark said. "I'm going to tell you. Then you have to pass it on to the others."

Steve frowned. "I don't know if I can—"

"There's no time! Even if you don't believe this or pray the prayer, you have to promise me you'll tell the others."

"I guess I can try."

"Good. You pray something like this from your heart: 'God, I know that I've sinned, and I'm sorry for that sin. I believe you sent Jesus, your only Son, to die in my place, and then he rose again three days later. . . .'"

Footsteps stopped in front of his cell. Someone unlocked the door.

"I ask you right now to forgive me, come into my life, and change me from the inside out. And help me not to give in to the evil one."

"Rebel," the guard yelled, "on your feet!"

"Do you have it?" Mark whispered.

Steve nodded. "I think so."

"Rebel!"

"One more thing," Mark said. "Afterward, you should be able to see something on their foreheads—that is, if you pray too."

"All right, we'll have to come in and get you," the guard said, taking a step toward Mark.

"And remember, tell them not to take Carpathia's—"

The guard jerked Mark to his feet by an arm, almost ripping it from its socket. Mark yelped and grabbed his shoulder as he was dragged from the cell. He looked back at Steve. "If they pray, God will give them the strength to face the blade." He turned to the others watching in stunned silence. "Give your lives to God right now! Don't wait!"

With that the guard threw Mark up against the wall. "There's only one God and it's Potentate Carpathia!" He kneed Mark, doubling him over, then put a gag in his mouth and pushed him through the door.

Mark glanced back but couldn't see Steve or any of the others. "God, I don't know if I gave them enough, but I pray you'd use what I said in their hearts," Mark prayed. "Help Steve, and give them the faith to see the truth and call out to you."

EIGHT

Interrogation

MARK was led into a room that had a table, three chairs, and a huge mirror on one wall. He guessed Commander Fulcire was watching from the other side but was surprised when the man entered and sat across the table from him.

Though Mark's leg wasn't hurting, his head and stomach ached from the guard's treatment.

"I was told you weren't cooperating in the cell," Fulcire said.

Mark stared at him.

Fulcire tossed a folder onto the table. Mark's mug shot was on top. "Your name is Mark Eisman. You attended Nicolae High in Mount Prospect. I suspect you were part of the underground that began the rebel newspaper at that school. You were known to be a friend of Vicki

Byrne, the same Vicki Byrne who killed her principal. Also known to the Global Community as Vicki B. She's been quite a burr under our saddle."

Mark was shocked.

Commander Fulcire ran a hand over the file and pulled out a page printed from the Young Trib Force's Web site. "We've pieced together some of your movements. The old schoolhouse, the fire in Wisconsin, the Stahley hideaway. Tell me, is the young girl—Darrion, I think her name was—still with your group, or did you leave her behind like you did the others?"

"What others?" Mark said.

Fulcire raised his eyebrows. "That got your attention, eh?" He pulled a picture of Natalie Bishop out of the pile and held it up. "This face ring a bell? Would you like to see what she looked like as she pleaded for her life? As she told us everything she knew about you?" He held up a gruesome photo of Natalie just after her execution.

"You're a monster," Mark mumbled.

"Excuse me? I didn't hear that last comment."

Mark clenched his teeth and tried to keep quiet, but his anger boiled over. "You will pay for the way you've treated followers of God."

"You mean followers of the false God. And I think the one who is about to pay is you."

"She was a sweet girl. You had no right to—"

"That 'sweet girl' helped several prisoners escape, gave vital Global Community information to our enemies, and was a wolf in sheep's clothing. But she became quite talkative near the end."

"Right, which is exactly what you're going to say about me, though I'm not going to give you any more information than she did."

Fulcire pursed his lips. "We can do this the easy way or the hard way. I suppose you prefer the more difficult path. Makes you feel like you're doing something noble, suffering like your so-called Messiah."

Fulcire nodded toward the door, and a guard walked behind Mark's chair. Mark braced himself for a blow to the head or body, but none came.

"There are ways to get the information we need," Fulcire said. "We don't have time to starve you. Things must move along a little quicker than that. We want to know about the others who were with you in the cabins."

Mark smiled. "I knew you hadn't caught them."

"So there were others . . ."

"Hundreds," Mark said. "And they all escaped by balloon."

Fulcire scowled and looked at the guard. Suddenly Mark felt pain in his right arm. The guard had stabbed him with a needle.

"This little concoction will be swimming through your bloodstream in a few minutes," Fulcire said. "We'll continue our discussion then, and I promise you will be more forthcoming."

Mark closed his eyes and shook his head. "It's working already. My head . . . it feels so light."

Fulcire squinted and leaned over the table.

"I'll tell you now," Mark gasped. "It wasn't a balloon. They took the yellow brick road to Oz."

Fulcire stood and glanced at the guard. The two walked out without speaking.

"Don't go yet," Mark pleaded, laughing. "I have more to tell you about the flying monkeys and the Tin Man."

As the door slammed, Mark's laughter turned to tears. The drug gave him a strange sensation.

" 'The Lord is my shepherd; I have everything I need,' " Mark whispered. " 'He lets me rest in green meadows; he leads me beside peaceful streams. He renews my strength. He guides me along right paths, bringing honor

to his name. Even when I walk through the
dark valley of death, I will not be afraid, for
you are close beside me. Your rod and your
staff protect and comfort me. . . .' "

Judd was excited to meet with Rayford Steele
and talk about the mission to Baghdad. Judd
had seen Rayford around Petra but hadn't
talked with him face-to-face.

Judd didn't expect to play a big part in the
Baghdad operation, but he and Vicki definitely wanted to be there. He had tinkered
with electronics when he was younger, and
he was sure he could help. And with Zeke's
ability to change people's appearances, there
was no way the GC would ever know who he
and Vicki really were.

Rayford met Judd and Vicki at the tech
center and moved to one of the high places
where Tsion and his elders had their meetings.
Rayford had aged a few years since Judd had
first seen him, and though his hair was turning a little gray, he was still in good shape.

"We've been praying for you and Buck and
Kenny," Vicki said as they sat.

"That means a lot to us," Rayford said.
"We know every day that passes brings us
closer to seeing her again, but it's hard. If we

didn't have the hope of heaven, I don't know what we'd do."

"You spoke with her before she died, right?" Judd said.

Rayford nodded. "I guess the GC was trying to trick her by having her call one of our secure numbers, but it backfired on them."

"How's that?" Vicki said.

"Well, after she gave me a message for Buck and Kenny, she told me she had been jogging near the San Diego hideout—which couldn't have been true. Chloe would never have been caught outside like that."

"What do you think she was doing?" Judd said.

"Trying to draw the GC away," Rayford said. "They were close to finding the others, and she was on watch that night."

"So how did her call backfire on the GC?" Vicki said.

"She mentioned something about a vacation our family had taken. I couldn't understand why talking about that was so important, and then I realized she was trying to tell me something. She said if she had one dream it would be that 'we could all go there right now, as soon as possible.' "

"She was talking about the others in the hideout?" Judd said.

"Yes. I didn't figure it out until later when Mac asked questions about that vacation. One of the places we went was Red Rocks, west of Denver. Mac made the connection about the red rocks of Petra, and we figured she meant we should get everybody over here pronto."

"Chloe was one of the smartest people I ever met," Vicki said.

Rayford smiled. "She said the same about you. Chloe told me once that you reminded her of her, just a few years younger."

Vicki blushed. "That's the best compliment I've ever received."

"Which makes what I'm about to say even more difficult," Rayford said. He took a breath. "We're not going to be using you in the Baghdad operation."

Judd gulped and looked away. "Can I ask why?"

"It was my decision. Chang and I have handpicked the team and feel we have the right amount of people. The GC has seen Vicki's picture, and we can assume they've seen yours as well. We don't need unnecessary risks."

"But *you're* going, aren't you?" Judd said.

"That's right."

"And you were on Carpathia's staff. That has to be a lot more dangerous than—"

Vicki put a hand on Judd's arm.

Captain Steele looked at the ground.

"I'm sorry," Judd said. "I don't mean to question your authority. We'll abide by whatever decision you make. And we'd be glad to help out here any way we can."

"I like that attitude."

After Rayford left, Judd and Vicki walked back to their home and talked about the situation. "I think we have to face the fact that Captain Steele is always going to think we're still just crazy teenagers," Judd said.

"I don't think he feels that way. Think of all the other people he didn't include in this operation. Our time will come."

"I just think we're going to be left out of the really good assignments."

"Which ones?" Vicki said.

Judd opened the door to their home and followed Vicki inside. He clicked on the computer screen and brought up a map of Israel. "This is the area where the Battle of Armageddon is going to be fought. And this is the spot where Jesus is supposed to come back."

"I know all that," Vicki said. "What's it got to do with us?"

"I want to be there, right in the middle of things and see it with my own eyes. I want to help fight the GC or at least support those who are trying to defend Jerusalem."

"And what about me?"

"I want you right there beside me." Judd took Vicki in his arms. "It'll be the greatest moment in the history of the world, and you and I are going to see it."

"One problem. How are we going to get there?"

Judd pushed Vicki a few inches away and looked at her. "I'll take care of that, but not a word about this to anybody. It's going to be our secret."

A few minutes after they gave Mark the shot, he felt woozy. *This must be what a numbskull feels like,* he thought.

He sat up and noticed someone standing in the corner by the one-way mirror. Mark leaned close and squinted. It was the angel from the bus.

"You're back?" Mark said.

The angel smiled and nodded. "You didn't finish the verses. The rest of the Psalm you were quoting."

"Oh, that," Mark said. "Where was I?"

"'You prepare a feast for me in the presence of my enemies. You welcome me as a guest, anointing my head with oil. My cup overflows with blessings.'"

Mark nodded and picked up the end of the verse. " 'Surely your goodness and unfailing love will pursue me all the days of my life, and I will live in the house of the Lord forever.' "

"That is what you can look forward to, my friend," the angel said.

Mark leaned back in his chair. "This stuff they gave me, will it make me talk?"

"You don't have to do anything you don't want to do. God will give you the strength to resist, no matter what they put into your veins. After all, as one of your hymn writers has said, 'The body they may kill; God's truth abideth still: His kingdom is forever.' "

"So I just shut my mouth and keep quiet?"

"Be creative."

Mark smiled. "Yeah, I'll try."

"They are almost ready to return. Before they do, I must tell you there was great rejoicing today."

"For what?"

"Because of you, because of the message, and because a few have gone from the kingdom of darkness to the kingdom of light."

"Steve," Mark whispered. "He told the others what I said?"

"He did, and they all believed in the only begotten Son of the Father, Jesus, the name that is above every name."

"How many?" Mark said.

Footsteps echoed down the hall.

"The ones who were appointed to believe have done so. You need not be concerned about the number. And now I will leave you."

"Please don't," Mark said. "Can't you stay and help me . . . do whatever I'm supposed to do?"

"If you truly need me, I'll be here," the angel said.

With that, the door opened and Commander Fulcire walked in with another man Mark hadn't seen before. When the door closed, Mark noticed the angel was gone.

Commander Fulcire looked closely at Mark and sat with a huge sandwich and onion rings. Barbecue sauce dripped from the bread, and Mark's stomach growled.

Fulcire took a bite of the sandwich and licked his fingers. "You know, it's amazing what the cooks here can do. A little information and we'll serve you a heaping plateful of some delicious food."

"I'm worried about your cholesterol," Mark said. "You really need to cut down on the fatty foods."

The other man sat near Fulcire and eyed Mark. "Let's start with something easy," he said.

"Who are you?" Mark said.

"Deputy Commander Lockerbie," the man said. "You're Mark Eisman, right?"

"If that's who you want me to be, that's who I am."

"It's not a question of who we want you to be but a quest for reality. Are you Mark Eisman?"

"Yes."

The man noted his answer and continued. "Are you part of the so-called Young Tribulation Force?"

"Yeah, I head up intramural sports."

"What was that?" Fulcire said.

"You know, basketball, football, badminton—that kind of thing. We tried to get a bowling team together, but we couldn't find an alley—"

"That's enough, Mr. Eisman," Fulcire said.

"Yeah, it was enough for us to go after a softball team. Had a hard time getting jerseys made up and an even harder time finding someone to play against."

"Enough!" Fulcire said.

"Have you ever participated in disloyal acts to the potentate?" Lockerbie said.

"No, not since I became a believer in him."

"Have you ever stolen anything to aid in your rebel acts?"

"Well, there was that satellite truck. I'm real sorry about that. I was going to fill it up with gas and return it, but I couldn't find you guys."

Lockerbie and Fulcire were not laughing, but Mark was having a good time. He looked past the men and saw his friend standing in the corner, chuckling.

"How am I doing so far?" Mark said to the angel.

Fulcire thought he was talking to him. "You won't be laughing when we take you to the blade."

"Probably not, but at least I'll know where I'm headed after my head's gone. You can kill my body, but you can't take my soul."

When Fulcire looked at the list of questions, Mark shook his head. "Look, Commander, I'm not going to tell you any more about my group because I don't know anything more. You probably want supply routes and locations of safe houses and that kind of stuff, and I'm just not going to give it up. So why don't we call this thing a bust? You sharpen your blade, and we can be done."

Lockerbie asked a few more questions, but Mark wouldn't say a word.

Finally Fulcire slammed his fist on the table and yelled, "Solitary!"

Mark was surprised he had gotten away without anyone trying to torture him. Would

that come later? When he made it to his
room, he collapsed on his cot and fell into a
deep sleep. He dreamed of streets paved with
gold.

NINE

Eyewitness Report

EARLY the next morning in Petra, Lionel made contact with Darrion and the others in Illinois and discovered they had found Lenore and her friends. Lionel wrote down their information and promised he would give them an update on Mark as soon as he heard anything.

"Jim Dekker, Colin Dial, and Conrad are talking about a rescue," Darrion said.

"I wouldn't recommend it," Lionel said. "If the info we're getting from Fulcire's computer is right, Mark is deep in the jail there. It would take a magician to get in and out."

Darrion said she would talk with the others and said good-bye.

Lionel had been glued to the computer for a long time, so he decided to take a walk. He found Sam Goldberg and Mr. Stein and explained the situation. The two were visibly upset and knelt where they were and prayed.

"Sovereign Lord, we ask you to send your ministering angels to encourage Mark right now," Mr. Stein prayed. "Prepare him for whatever you have planned."

After they had prayed, Sam took Lionel to meet his friend Lev Taubman and his mother. They had become believers shortly after family members had died in a rebellion.

"Lev has been in touch with some friends in Jerusalem," Sam said.

"Believers?" Lionel said.

Lev shook his head. "But they have not taken the mark of Carpathia. They say they are going to fight with rebel forces against Carpathia. They want to save Jerusalem."

"That'll be like a peewee football team trying to win against an NFL team," Lionel said.

"What?" Sam said.

"They're going to lose the battle, and they'll probably all be killed."

"I know that," Sam said. "But Lev and I think we might be able to reach some of them for God. We want to go to Jerusalem before the big battle and tell them the truth."

After hearing their plan, Lionel thought he should tell Judd and Vicki about this new development.

Mark sat alone in the darkness and waited. He could have played the interrogation a little better and made them think he was giving them solid information, but he was tired of playing.

His cell was down the hall and around the corner from the other prisoners. He felt something crawling on him and stood and flailed his arms. He settled on the cot and pulled a lone blanket around his shoulders.

Through the hall came singing, but Mark couldn't make out the words. Then another voice joined in and another. There had to be at least half a dozen people singing now.

Mark put his ear to the door. He heard the word *Jesus* in the song, slid to the floor, and closed his eyes. He thought of little Ryan, the Fogartys' son. How many times had Mark helped put him down for a nap singing "Jesus Loves Me"? That was one of Ryan's favorites, and he always asked Mark to sing it again and again.

A soft glow filled the room, and Mark greeted the angel. The being looked at him kindly and sat. Mark couldn't believe he was so comfortable with this heavenly visitor.

"What was that singing?" Mark said.

"I was teaching your friends a new song," the angel said.

"Were they scared of you?"

"No. And they learned the words quickly."

"What about the unbelievers? They must have been afraid."

The angel smiled. "They managed to fall into a deep sleep."

"That happens a lot with you, doesn't it?" Mark said. "Those guards on the bus did the same thing when you came around."

The angel smiled again.

"What song did you teach them?"

The angel closed his eyes and began singing in a low, pleasing voice.

> *"What can wash away my sin?*
> *Nothing but the blood of Jesus;*
> *What can make me whole again?*
> *Nothing but the blood of Jesus.*
> *Oh! precious is the flow*
> *That makes me white as snow;*
> *No other fount I know,*
> *Nothing but the blood of Jesus."*

"That's good. You should get a band together and go on the road."

"We lift our voices in praise every day, but I must say, the words of the hymn writers are unique."

"What do you mean?" Mark said.

"Humans write about redemption, salvation, the power in the blood of Jesus. We angels know nothing about such things, other than what we observe. We cannot be 'saved,' as you would call it. We had one chance to follow or rebel and that was it."

"You mean when Satan was cast out of heaven?" Mark said.

"Correct. One third of the host of heaven followed Lucifer, and the others remained faithful to the Almighty. But all humans have fallen. All of them have sinned and fallen short of the glory of God."

"I guess I've never really thought about it that way. So why did we get a second chance and you didn't?"

The angel took a breath, as if he were smelling a sweet flower for the first time. "The grace of God," he whispered. "We look at it and are encouraged. We see it at work and are in awe of the plan of the Lord. He became one of you, a kinsman redeemer—a person who was in every way like you, except that this person was without sin. Jesus, who was God, became human. . . . I was there, you know."

"Where?"

"Bethlehem, on the hills overlooking the town. You should have seen those shepherds when we started singing." The angel paused. "But I tell you too much."

"No, please don't stop," Mark said.

The angel put his hands on his knees. "We didn't know what to think, the Son of God coming to earth as a helpless baby. That he would submit to such a life, then give himself as a sacrifice on Golgotha." The angel shuddered. "Such an ugly death."

"You were there?"

"The Son could have called on us at any moment, and we would have taken him from that place." He held out a fist. "We would have struck down those Romans like toy soldiers. But he didn't call on us. He took the shame and the beatings and the nails." He shook his head. "How can you understand? How can any being comprehend such love?"

Mark bit his lip. "Can you teach me the song? I went to church, but I don't really remember it."

The angel spoke the words again, then picked up the melody and Mark sang along. When he heard the words, Mark found he could memorize them immediately. Tears rimmed his eyes as he reached the next verse.

> "Now by this I'll overcome—
> Nothing but the blood of Jesus;
> Now by this I'll reach my home—

> *Nothing but the blood of Jesus.*
> *Oh! precious is the flow*
> *That makes me white as snow;*
> *No other fount I know,*
> *Nothing but the blood of Jesus."*

Footsteps approached and the angel stood, his nostrils flaring.

"Is this it?" Mark said.

"I'm not sure. From what I can tell, there may be one more test of your will. But stand strong, my friend. You are a child of the King, and you will soon be home."

The door opened and Mark scooted to avoid it.

Deputy Commander Lockerbie walked through with another guard. "This way, Eisman."

They led Mark through a series of hallways. He had no idea what time it was, but when the deputy commander took him outside, the cool, brisk air hit him in the face and Mark breathed deeply. The moon shone brightly in the cloudless sky.

Across the courtyard was a row of wooden tables, dwarfed by several guillotines. Mark had seen this setup on live feeds from GC prisons around the world. Some of the highest rated programs on television were rebel executions. Mark hadn't watched many of these, but the ones he had seen had turned his stomach.

In spite of the cool weather, flies buzzed around them. The smell was overpowering. Several huge trash bins stood alongside the main building.

The deputy commander excused the guard and turned to Mark. "This is where it happens. Unless you cooperate, tomorrow you'll be out here."

"This is where I'll wind up no matter what I say and you know it."

"Not necessarily. You give us information on pilots, supply routes, locations of hiding places, information like that, and we'll make things easier." Lockerbie had a kind face, not unlike Mark's cousin John. In fact, the two looked remarkably alike. "We have information that your group has been in contact with the mole inside the palace in New Babylon. Do you know anything about that?"

"Look, I can help in a lot of ways, but if the palace has a mole, I'd suggest you get an exterminator or a trap. I don't know much about catching small animals."

"Not that kind of mole. You know what I'm talking about."

"You get nothing from me," Mark said.

The deputy commander turned Mark

around and keys jangled. Soon Mark's hands were free. He rubbed his wrists to get the circulation going again. "Why'd you do that?"

Lockerbie sighed. "Not all of us in here are the monsters you think we are. We do have some compassion."

"You mean like a nice meal before you slice my neck?"

"No, I can see that you live. Simply take the mark and we'll put you in a cell of your own. After this all dies down you can be moved and have more privileges. I'll even find a Bible for you."

"Right, like I really believe you're going to come through on all that."

Lockerbie dug into his pocket and frowned. "They would have *my* head if they knew I was doing this, but I had a younger brother. He was killed in the outbreak of poison gas. You remind me of him." He handed Mark a cell phone. "I'm going to let you stay out here for a while. You won't be able to run. There's razor wire all around, and the guards are armed. But think about your life and what it's worth. Call someone you know, someone who cares for you. I'll be back in a few minutes."

Mark took the phone and studied it as the deputy commander slipped inside. *What an obvious trick! The GC wants me to call my friends—any number they can trace. The phone might even have a bug in it so they can listen.*

Mark ambled over to a wooden table and glanced at a guard high in a tower. The ground was wet with dew. He sat on the table and studied a guillotine. The contraption disgusted him and he turned away.

Who could he call? No way was he going to dial Conrad, Shelly, or the others. He also didn't want to call Petra. Though he longed to talk with Judd, Lionel, or Vicki, he didn't want to mess up and have them give information the GC wanted.

Then he got an idea. A truly inspired idea. *The angel will like this one*, Mark thought.

Lionel hit the Record button while he watched the latest news from the United North American States. He had asked Naomi to get Judd and Vicki.

An anchorwoman named April Wojekowski held one hand to her ear as she searched for words. "I'm told that you're one of the rebels captured by Commander Fulcire in last night's raid, is that correct?"

"You got that right," a young man said.

The voice sounded familiar. Could it be Mark?

"That commander is a tough bird. He's been asking me lots of questions, and I've been giving him lots of answers."

It is Mark!

"Is that so?" Wojekowski said.

"Yeah, they gave me one phone call, and I thought I'd make it to the media so you could have the story."

"And what story is that?"

"I was part of a group called the Young Tribulation Force that started an underground Web site. We wanted people to know about the Global Community because we thought it was bad. Now, after talking with Commander Fulcire and the others here, I know the truth."

"So the commander has set you straight?"

"Right."

Lionel's heart sank. Was Mark giving the GC information? Had they somehow brainwashed him? Judd and Vicki ran in and Lionel put a finger to his lips. "Mark's on the phone with GCNN."

Mark had slowly moved behind the huge trash bins, being careful the guard in the tower didn't notice him. He hid, choking at the awful smell, hoping this would be the last place anyone would look.

He had gotten the GCNN phone number from the directory of the deputy commander's cell phone. He hadn't expected to actually get on the air, but when it happened he prayed God would keep him calm.

"What have you told Commander Fulcire that you'd like to share with us?" Wojekowski said.

The door to the courtyard banged open, and several guards poured out.

Mark held the phone close, took a deep breath, and spoke softly. "Actually, I haven't even shared this with the commander, so you'll be the first to know." He imagined the woman looking into the camera and sitting a little taller in her chair. "To all those who have read our Web site, or who were interested in knowing why the disappearances happened, or why we've had all these natural disasters, like the darkness in New Babylon, I'd like to point them to Dr. Tsion Ben-Judah's Web site." Mark gave the address quickly before the woman cut him off.

"So the commander hasn't really changed your mind about being against Potentate Carpathia?"

Footsteps getting closer. Voices yelling.

"Being in here and seeing how they treat prisoners makes me all the more determined to live my last breath for Jesus Christ," Mark said.

"Behind the garbage bins!" a guard shouted.

"Judd, Vicki, Lionel, Conrad—and anybody who's listening—I'm not alone in here! I'm all right. And I'll see you on the other side!"

The phone clicked and Mark wondered if his friends had heard his last few words.

Someone shoved a gun barrel into Mark's back and he stood. Deputy Commander Lockerbie snatched the phone away and led him back to his cell.

TEN

The Blade

THE next few minutes were agony for Judd and the others watching from Petra. Judd put himself in Mark's place and pictured the GC leading him straight to the guillotine.

It was Vicki's idea to pray, and Naomi Tiberius ran for her father, an elder at Petra. She returned with him and Chaim Rosenzweig.

"Dear ones," Chaim said softly, "let us join together."

For the next hour the group gave thanks to God for Mark—for all the things he had done to help people come to know Jesus and for the good friend he had been.

"Father, we ask that you give special comfort and strength to Mark right now," Chaim prayed. "Stir his heart and give him a peace that passes all understanding."

When Eleazar Tiberius spoke, his voice boomed in the tech center, and many of the workers stopped what they were doing and gathered around. Judd didn't even know most of them, but he could tell they sensed one of their brothers was in trouble.

"Sovereign Lord, we knew when this period of Tribulation began that many would die for your sake," Mr. Tiberius prayed. "And though we would ask for a miracle, it may be your will that Mark passes through this fire rather than being taken out of it. So I ask you to bring to his mind what the psalmist said: 'Lord, give to me your unfailing love, the salvation that you promised me. Then I will have an answer for those who taunt me, for I trust in your word. Do not snatch your word of truth from me, for my only hope is in your laws.' "

Vicki wept as she prayed. "Father, you know how much Mark and I disagreed, but I never doubted that he wanted to follow you as much as anyone. Whatever's happening to him right now, help him remember all of his friends and how much we love him."

"Yes, Father," Chang prayed. "Because of you and your love, none of us is ever alone. We thank you for friendships and the chance to join in the sufferings of our brother Mark. If we could take his place, we would do that, but you have called him to face this final task and you would not choose someone who would fail you. We give you thanks and pray you would hold Mark up even now."

Mark came back to consciousness, not knowing how long he had been in his darkened cell. He groped his way across the floor until he reached the cot. He felt his head and found a lump the size of a Ping-Pong ball. His back ached, and he wondered how many guards had joined in the capture.

He wished his angel friend would return. He would have to ask his name this time. How good of God to send a final companion.

Verses flooded Mark's mind, especially from the Psalms. Then he recalled Jesus in the Garden of Gethsemane and his prayer to God to 'take this cup of suffering away from me.' Jesus' mental anguish had been so intense that the Bible said he had sweat great drops of blood. Suddenly Mark could understand that a little better.

"God, thanks for letting me go through this. I wouldn't have chosen it, but if this is what you want me to do, I want to be faithful."

Mark thought of Jesus' crucifixion. He had been tortured and killed. Dying on the cross took hours of agony. Mark's would be over in seconds—at least that's what he hoped.

"What are you thinking, my friend?" someone said.

Mark looked up. It was the angel, standing in a corner, shining with a heavenly light. "You mean you can't read my mind?" Mark said.

"Only the Almighty can see into your heart. We can only guess."

"I'm just trying to think straight," Mark said. "Could I ask your name?"

"You may call me Caleb."

"Have you done this many times?"

Caleb nodded. "There have been more in the past few months than ever."

"Does anybody . . . I mean, when it comes time to . . . you know . . ."

"God's people have always acted with great courage. Some weep at the end, others sing, and some quote Scripture. It is different every time, and yet there are remarkable similarities."

"Like what?"

"The looks on their faces. The hope that shines through. Those who are doing the killing look like shells, but the ones being executed are truly alive. It happened that way recently with Chloe Williams. She was able to speak of the living Christ before her death."

"You visited Chloe?"

Caleb put a hand over his chest. "Her heart was breaking over leaving her husband and son, but she expressed her desire to be with Jesus."

"Will you do the same thing you did in the courtyard when Chloe was executed? You know, the bright shimmering thing we saw on TV?"

Caleb smiled. "Each event is different. If there is need for me to be there and speak, I will." He tilted his head slightly to the left and gazed at Mark. "Thus says the Son of the most high God: 'I am the resurrection and the life. He who believes in Me, though he may die, yet shall he live. And whoever lives and believes in Me shall never die.' Be comforted by these words."

Mark raised his eyebrows. "Thank you. I hope I won't let you down."

The angel stepped closer. "I know you won't because you are one of his."

Mark took a deep breath. His throat caught and he had trouble speaking. "Well, I don't know how to thank you for coming and helping me get through this. I suppose you have other things you could be doing—angel stuff."

Footsteps echoed down the hallway.

Caleb smiled again. " 'Peace I leave with you,' says your Lord Christ. 'My peace I give you, not as the world gives, give I unto you. Let not your heart be troubled, neither let it be afraid.' "

And Caleb was gone.

Commander Fulcire stepped into the room, accompanied by several guards. Mark thought it odd the deputy commander wasn't there.

When Mark stepped from the prison, the first rays of light peeked over the horizon. A long, thin cloud tinged with yellow hung in the sky. The way the sun hit it made it look almost golden. A jet sped high in the sky leaving a white trail. It intersected the cloud and came out the other side. Mark couldn't help thinking the whole thing looked like a cross.

Mark expected the same kind of fanfare as Chloe, news trucks lined up, the works. But there weren't even people manning the tables at this hour. A few guards huddled together, trying to keep warm.

Fulcire pushed Mark to the first guillotine and turned. "Bring out the others."

After a few moments, six men were led from the jail. Mark recognized Steve at the front of the group with the mark of the believer on his forehead. The others all had the same mark.

Commander Fulcire pulled a cell phone from his pocket and dialed a number.

Steve smiled and stood close to Mark. "I was afraid you'd be gone before they brought us out here."

"Me too," Mark said. "You must have remembered all I said."

"It's funny. I knew everything you told me, even believed it. I knew God was doing all the stuff around us, but I always thought I was too far gone to turn around."

"We want to thank you," another man said to Mark. "I think God brought you to us."

Mark nodded. "I think you're right." He looked at Steve. "But why did they single you guys out this morning?"

Steve's eyes twinkled. "We all said we didn't want you to be alone. We told the guards we would never bow down to Carpathia or take his mark, and if they were going to use these—" he nodded toward the guillotines— "that we wanted to be with you."

Mark shook his head and bit his lip to keep from crying. "You didn't have to do that."

"You didn't have to come to us, and you didn't have to risk telling us your message," another man whispered. "But you did."

"That reminds me of a verse in the Bible, a couple actually," Mark said. "Paul says something about being thankful to God every time he thinks of the people he's writing. He says, 'I always pray for you, and I make my requests with a heart full of joy because you have been my partners in spreading the Good News about Christ from the time you first heard it until now.'

"You guys haven't been believers long, but you have been faithful to what God called you. The next verse says, 'And I am sure that God, who began the good work within you, will continue his work until it is finally finished on that day when Christ Jesus comes back again.' That day is coming real soon, but we're going to see him sooner.

"When Jesus hung on the cross, just before he died, he said to a man next to him, 'Today you will be with me in paradise.' Well, I believe that the moment we leave this life, we're going to see him, and you'll see that the little bit of suffering we had to go through here will really be worth it."

"A man came to us and taught us a song," another man said.

"That was an angel," Mark said.

The men's eyes widened.

"I didn't see any wings," Steve said.

Commander Fulcire stepped forward and faced Mark. "You have some kind of feeling for these prisoners?"

"They're my brothers," Mark choked.

"Quaint. Well, I'll give you one more

chance. What you say now could save the life of your 'brothers,' as you call them. I will allow them to go back to their cells and live if you'll tell us what we want to know."

Mark wanted to tell Commander Fulcire the truth a final time. He wanted to scream at him that Jesus was coming back and would conquer the armies of the Antichrist. Instead, Mark felt compassion for the man who had followed the devil.

"I feel sorry for you," Mark whispered.

Fulcire laughed. *"You* feel sorry for *me?"*

"One day every person on earth will admit that Jesus Christ is Lord. He is the true Potentate and the Creator of the universe."

"So you don't want to save your friends?"

"One day soon, New Babylon is going to be destroyed."

"Impossible."

"And the armies of your leader will go to battle against God's people."

"I hope to be there," Fulcire said.

"You and those like you who wear the uniform of the Global Community will be struck down."

"With all the weaponry and firepower at our disposal? Not likely."

Mark looked at the guards with Fulcire. "Do anything you can to stay away from the last battle. Get sick. Run away. But don't be near Israel in six months."

The guards scoffed. Fulcire motioned, and two guards led Steve to the guillotine. "Last chance to save this man's life," the commander said.

Steve looked back at Mark. "I've already been saved. Can you guys sing one more time?"

The others began the song Caleb had taught them. As they sang the verse, "'This is all my hope and peace, Nothing but the blood of Jesus; This is all my righteousness, Nothing but the blood of Jesus,'" the blade fell and Steve died.

One by one the guards led the others in front of Mark to the guillotine. The guards tried to stop them from singing, and several men went to the guillotine with missing teeth, but they kept singing to the end.

Fulcire saved Mark for last. As the guards picked up the body of the man before him and moved it, the commander pushed Mark toward the blood-caked machine. "Look around you, Eisman. No masses of people to preach to. No flashing lights of supposed angels. You die alone, and you die now."

Mark felt a sense of peace flowing, like the prayers of his friends were lifting him. Faces flashed in his mind—Judd's, Vicki's, Lionel's,

Ryan's, and many others. He had fought the good fight. He hadn't done everything perfectly, and he had done some stupid things, but God had used him.

He knelt on the blood-soaked ground. *Holy ground*, he thought. *Ground soaked by the blood of the martyrs*.

Caleb's song came to him and he sang it softly. " 'Now by this I'll overcome—Nothing but the blood of Jesus, Now by this I'll reach my home—Nothing but the blood of Jesus. Oh! precious is the flow that makes me white as snow; No other fount I know, Nothing but the blood of Jesus.' "

With his eyes fixed on the ground, Mark breathed a final prayer knowing that at any second he would be in the presence of God.

"Into your hands I commit my spirit," he whispered.

"Good riddance, Judah-ite," Fulcire said.

A lever tripped.

Something clunked, and Mark felt the machine shudder as the blade plunged.

A millisecond before it hit his neck, Mark thought he heard rustling wings and singing.

Then a flash of light.

And he was in heaven.

ELEVEN

Tsion's Message

FOR the next several days Judd moved around Petra in a fog. He kept replaying first meeting Mark and John at Nicolae High and all the things they had been through. Though Vicki talked openly about Mark's death, Judd found it difficult. He knew that frustrated Vicki, but it was taking him longer to accept the truth. Mark was gone.

As Vicki played with Kenny in their house, Judd took a walk to one of the high places and sat. He asked God to help him understand what had happened. Within minutes, an ovation arose in the distance. As Judd made his way carefully down the mountainside, he heard the voice of Tsion Ben-Judah echo off the rock walls.

Judd had heard from Lionel that Tsion planned to go live on international television with Chang's help. Judd wondered what Carpathia and his goons would think of that. Tsion was speaking to not only a million in Petra but billions worldwide.

When Judd arrived at the massive gathering, Tsion was already well into his message. He explained that the truth of God's Word was confirmed by the judgments and plagues. From the disappearances to the hail and fire, the burning mountain that fell into the sea, to the demonic locusts—all these and more were proof that God's Word was true.

". . . Two more judgments await before the glorious appearing of our Lord and Savior, Jesus the Christ," Tsion was saying to the people and a nearby camera. "Hear me! The Euphrates River will become as dry land! Scoff today but be amazed when it happens, and remember it was foretold. The last judgment will be an earthquake that levels the entire globe. This judgment will bring hail so huge it will kill millions.

"I am asked every day, how can people see all these things and still choose Antichrist over Christ? It is the puzzle of the ages. For many of you, it is already too late to change your mind. You may now see that you have chosen the wrong side in this war. But if you pledged your allegiance to the enemy of God by taking his mark of loyalty, it is too late for you.

"If you have not taken the mark yet, it may *still* be too late, because you waited so long. You pushed the patience of God past the breaking point.

"But there may be a chance for you. You will know only if you pray to receive Christ, tell God you recognize that you are a sinner and separated from him, and that you acknowledge that your only hope is in the blood of Christ, shed on the cross for you.

"Remember this: If you do not turn to Christ and are not saved from the coming judgment, this awful earth you endure right now is as good as your life will ever get. If you do turn to Christ and your heart has not already been hardened, this world is the worst you'll see for the rest of eternity.

"For those of you who are already my brothers and sisters in Christ around the world, I urge you to be faithful unto death, for Jesus himself said, 'Do not fear any of those things which you are about to suffer. Indeed, the devil is about to throw some of you into prison, that you may be tested. . . . Be faithful until death, and I will give you the crown of life.'

"What a promise! Christ himself will give

you the crown of life. It shall be a thrill to see Jesus come yet again, but oh, what a privilege to die for his sake."

Judd sat on a rock and thought about Mark. He had earned the crown of life! Even now he could be in the presence of Jesus, worshiping and praising God. Judd missed the next few moments of Tsion's message, then focused on the man's words as he spoke of things to come.

"Now I must tell you there is also bad news," Tsion said. "The wrath of the evil one will reach a fever pitch from now until the end. There will be increasing demands for all people to worship him and take his mark. To you who share my faith and are willing to be faithful unto death, remember the promise in James 5:8 that 'the coming of the Lord is at hand.'

"Oh, believer, share your faith and live your life boldly in such a way that others can receive Christ by faith and be saved. Think of it, friend. You could pray to be led to those who have not yet heard the truth. You may be the one who leads the very last soul to Christ.

"Second Peter 3:10-14 says that 'the day of the Lord will come as a thief in the night, in which the heavens will pass away with a great noise, and the elements will melt with fervent heat; both the earth and the works that are in it will be burned up.

" 'Therefore, since all these things will be dissolved, what manner of persons ought you to be in holy conduct and godliness, looking for and hastening the coming of the day of God, because of which the heavens will be dissolved, being on fire, and the elements will melt with fervent heat? Nevertheless we, according to His promise, look for new heavens and a new earth in which righteousness dwells.

" 'Therefore, beloved, looking forward to these things, be diligent to be found by Him in peace, without spot and blameless.'

"I urge you to imitate our Lord and Savior and say with him, 'I must be about My Father's business.' "

As Tsion continued, Judd felt a new resolve to serve God. No matter what it cost him, no matter where he had to go, he wanted to be about God's business.

Tsion urged viewers to visit his Web site for more information and to decide for Christ. "The most wonderful news I can share with you today is that God has prompted us to use the brilliant minds and technology we have been blessed with here. Anyone who communicates with us via the

Internet will get a personal response with everything you need to know about how to receive Christ.

"Yes, I know the ruler of this world has outlawed even visiting our site, but we can assure you that it is secure and that your visit cannot be traced. We have thousands of Internet counselors who can answer any question and lead you to Christ.

"We also have teams of rescuers who can transport you here if you are being persecuted for the sake of Christ. This is a dangerous time, and many will be killed. Many of our own loved ones have lost their lives in the pursuit of righteousness. But we will do what we can until the end to keep fighting for what is right. For in the end, we win, and we will be with Jesus."

Tsion's words warmed Judd's heart, and as he walked home he prayed for the people who would see the broadcast and who hadn't accepted the mark of Carpathia. He believed everything Tsion had said, but there was still an ache in his heart about Mark.

Lionel saw Judd a few days after Tsion had spoken and called him over. "You don't think Mark's death is your fault, do you?"

Judd winced. "I know I couldn't have done anything to save him, but I don't understand why he was so stupid."

"He saved the others. That wasn't stupid."

"Not that. The way Mark was, going with the militia, doing stuff without thinking about the consequences."

"You mean you're upset because he was so much like you?" Lionel said.

Judd stared at him.

"I'm serious," Lionel said. "Mark was always doing stuff without talking with others, getting an idea and running with it. Sometimes it worked out. Sometimes it didn't."

Judd shook his head. "Maybe I'm mad because he didn't change."

"And maybe this whole Baghdad thing— that you didn't get to go with Captain Steele— has something to do—"

"It's not that," Judd snapped. He turned away and looked at a row of screens with people typing messages. "You know what really ticks me off? That God let it happen in the first place."

"Okay, so that's who you're really mad at."

"Why does he allow his followers to die like that? Thousands have been executed by the GC. Thousands! And God just sits there or stands or whatever."

"Remember when my uncle André died?" Lionel said. "I thought I had a good chance to tell him the truth. I was ticked off at God for a long time about that."

"How'd you resolve it?"

Lionel scratched his head and patted the stump of his left arm. "Same way I resolved this. There are some things I'm just not going to understand. God lets some things happen that don't make sense, at least to me. But I guess part of faith is believing that God is still on the throne and that none of this is taking him by surprise."

Judd sat and heaved a sigh. "When I was little one of my uncles died. He was a strong Christian and used to take me on sailing trips on Lake Michigan. I couldn't understand how God could let such a good guy get cancer and die. I still don't see any sense in it, even though I believe God's there and really does care."

"I like to think that God was so near to Mark at the end," Lionel said, "that Mark could have gone through anything. It's clear from the communication from Fulcire that Mark didn't give them a thing."

"Though the reporters said he blabbed everything."

Lionel clicked on the computer and pulled up messages from readers to Tsion Ben-

Judah's Web site. Tsion had allowed Lionel
and the others to put a section for the Young
Trib Force there, and Vicki had written a trib-
ute to Mark.

"Mark worked so hard on different parts of
the Web site," Lionel said, "and there are
people who are believers today because of
what he did. And if he were here right now, I
think he'd want us to keep doing everything
we can to reach out to people."

"That's my goal too, but there's something
else that's come up since his death."

"What's that?"

Judd lowered his voice. "Vicki and I want
to be in Jerusalem when the final war starts."

"You're crazy."

"We want to make life miserable for those
GC troops that'll try to overrun the city and
then be there when Jesus comes back and
wins the battle with only a few words."

"You're both going to get killed."

"So, if that's what God wants . . ."

"Don't let your anger at Fulcire and his
goons make you go off the deep end. When
the GC get here, they're going to unleash
everything they have. If you're in the way—"

"I have to be in the way," Judd snapped.

Lionel rubbed his neck. "You haven't seen
the video from Baghdad yet, have you?"

"I wasn't invited to see it."

Lionel caught Chang's attention and asked if he could show Judd a clip of the conference. Chang showed Lionel where to find the file, and Lionel pulled it up on the screen. "This is the creepiest thing I've seen from Carpathia. And if he's going to be in Jerusalem when the end comes, it's one place I **don't** want to be, and I don't want you to be. I hope seeing this will help you change your mind. If Vicki's going with you—"

"Just show me the video," Judd said.

"All right, but let me set it up. Captain Steele and the others put bugs in the conference room where they knew Nicolae and his cabinet would meet. Before his heads of state got there, Carpathia hinted to his top people that something big was up."

"More beheadings of believers?"

"No, though that's happening. He said he wanted to introduce his people to a trio who would help accomplish their goals. Leon Fortunato and the others begged to hear more, but Carpathia wouldn't tell them. Then when they had their big meeting . . . well, let me just show you." Lionel fast-forwarded the video. "I'm showing you this so you know what kind of evil you're dealing with. Are you ready?"

Judd nodded and prepared himself for the worst.

TWELVE

The Evil Trio

VICKI walked into the tech center and spotted Judd looking over Lionel's shoulder. Judd still hadn't been able to talk much about Mark, but she was trying to be patient.

"Hello, Mrs. Thompson," Chang said with a smile.

Vicki couldn't get used to hearing the words *Mrs. Thompson*. It made her feel old. "Please call me Vicki."

Judd waved Vicki over and explained what they were watching. He seemed more excited than he had for days as he told her what was happening on the screen. Lionel started the video over, and Vicki stared at the surprisingly clear footage.

Vicki had seen news reports about the arrival of the ten regional potentates to Baghdad and the resulting parades, light shows, and stage shows performed in their honor. Stands filled with people cheered each regional potentate. It was more than Vicki could stand to watch the unholy mockery.

Leon Fortunato had introduced Nicolae, and the crowd had interrupted him many times with huge ovations. Most chilling was Carpathia's pledge to eliminate those who opposed peace, as he put it, within half a year.

Interesting timing, Vicki thought.

"This meeting took place the morning after Carpathia's big speech about killing their enemies," Lionel said. "Nobody saw this except for the people in that room in Baghdad and those who were handpicked by Rayford Steele here in Petra."

"Amazing," Vicki said as she studied the video. She saw a nervous Leon Fortunato and several potentates, including the one from the United North American States. She also noticed Suhail Akbar, chief of Security and Intelligence.

"You can see they're each wearing clothing from their region," Judd said, pointing to the African and South American potentates who wore colorful outfits.

"Who are those three?" Vicki said. "They look like statues."

Lionel nodded. "Just wait. You'll see."

The three didn't move an inch. They

seemed to be staring at the wall in front of them and didn't even react when Carpathia walked into the room.

Vicki shuddered. "They give me the creeps."

"Let me jump to the place where Carpathia begins." Lionel found the spot, and Judd scooted a chair close so Vicki could sit.

Nicolae thanked the group for coming and told them he was the boss. He reminded them that three potentates from the group had died untimely deaths. His message was clear: Either follow me or die.

"Questions?" Nicolae said. "I thought not. Let us proceed."

"This is where it gets good," Lionel said. "I mean, not good, but . . . you know what I mean."

"Ladies and gentlemen," Carpathia said, "the time has come for me to take you into my confidence. We must all be on the same page in order to win the ultimate battle. Look into my eyes and listen, because what you hear today is truth and you will have no trouble believing every word of it. I am eternal. I am from everlasting to everlasting. I was there at the beginning, and I will remain through eternity future."

Nicolae stood and began to slowly circle the table.

"It's as if they're in a trance," Vicki said. "Like they're scared to even look at him."

"Here is the problem," Carpathia continued. "The one who calls himself God is not God. I will concede that he preceded me. When I evolved out of the primordial ooze and water, he was already there. But plainly, he had come about in the same manner I did. Simply because he preceded me, he wanted me to think he created me and all the other beings like him in the vast heavens. I knew better. Many of us did."

Vicki looked at Judd and shook her head. "I can't believe he's really saying this."

Carpathia talked as if he were explaining a math problem to a group of second graders. "He tried to tell us we were created as ministering servants. We had a job to do. He said he had created humans in his own image and that we were to serve them. Had I been there first, I could have told *him* that I had created *him* and that it was *he* who would serve me by ministering to my other creations.

"But he did not create anything! We, all of us—you, me, the other heavenly hosts, men and women—all came from that same primordial soup. But no! Not according to him! He was there with another evolved being like myself, and he claimed that one as his favored son. He was the special one, the chosen one, the only begotten one.

"I knew from the beginning it was a lie and that I—all of us—was being used. I was a bright and shining angel. I had ambition. I had ideas. But that was threatening to the older one. He called himself the creator God, the originator of life. He took the favored position. He demanded that the whole earth worship and obey him. I had the audacity to ask why. Why not me?"

"Because you're the father of lies," Judd said under his breath.

Carpathia admitted he had started a rebellion against God. "About a third of the other evolved beings agreed with me and took my side, promised to remain loyal. The other two-thirds were weaklings, easily swayed. They took the side of the so-called father and his so-called son."

"Is he talking about the angels?" Judd said.

"He has to be," Vicki said. "In Revelation it talks about a third of the stars being cast down to earth with Lucifer."

Carpathia continued, saying he would go back to heaven where he was before he was cast out. "We have been mortal enemies ever since, that father and that son and I. He even persuaded the evolved humans that he created them! But that could not be true, because if he had, they would not have free will. And if he created me, I would not have been able to rebel. It only makes sense.

"Once I figured that out, I began enjoying my role as the outcast. I found humans, the ones he liked to call his own, the easiest to sway. The woman with the fruit! She did not want to obey. It took nothing, mere suggestion, to get her to do what she really wanted. That happened not far from right here, by the way."

Carpathia walked around the group, lecturing them and giving his spin on the Bible. This was the gospel of the Antichrist, and the people in the room seemed to drink it in.

"And the first human siblings—they were easy! The younger was devoted to the one who called himself the only true God, but the other . . . ah, the other wanted only what I wanted. A little something for himself. Before you know it, I am proving beyond doubt that these creatures are not really products of the older angel's creativity. Within a few generations I have them so confused, so selfish, so full of themselves that the old man no longer wants to claim they were made in his image.

"They get drunk; they fight; they blaspheme. They are stubborn; they are unfaithful. They kill each other. The only ones I cannot get through to are Noah and his kin. Of course, the great creator decides the rest of history depends on them and wipes out everyone else with a flood. I eventually got to Noah, but he had already started repopulating the earth.

"Yes, I will admit it. The father and the son have been formidable foes over the generations. They have their favorites—the Jews, of all people. The Jews are the apples of the elder's eye, but therein lies his weakness. He has such a soft spot for them that they will be his undoing.

"My forces and I almost had them wiped out not so many generations ago, but father and son intervened, gave them back their own land, and foiled us again. Fate has toyed with us many times, my friends, but in the end we shall prevail.

"Father and son thought they were doing the world a favor by putting their intentions in writing. The whole plan is there, from sending the son to die and resurrect—which I proved I could do as well—to foretelling this entire period. Yes, many millions bought into this great lie. Up to now I would have to acknowledge that the other side has had the advantage.

"But two great truths will be their undoing. First, I know the truth. They are not greater or better than I or anyone else. They came from the same place we all did. And second, they must not have realized that I can read. I read their book! I know what they are up to! I know what happens next, and I even know where!

"Let them turn the lights off in the great city that I loved so much! Ah, how beautiful it was when it was the center for commerce and government, and the great ships and planes brought in goods from all over the globe. So it is dark now. And so what if it is eventually destroyed? I will build it back up, because I am more powerful than father and son combined.

"Let them shake the earth until it is level and drop hundred-pound chunks of ice from the skies. I will win in the end because I have read their battle plan. The old man plans to send the son to set up the kingdom he predicted more than three hundred times in his book, and he even tells where he will land! Ladies and gentlemen, we will have a surprise waiting for him."

Lionel stopped the recording. "See what I mean?"

"He actually thinks he can beat God," Judd said. "Incredible."

Lionel went forward on the recording and hit Play.

"We rally everyone—all of our tanks and planes and weapons and armies—in the Plain of Megiddo," Nicolae said. "It is in the Plain of Esdraelon in northern Israel, about twenty miles southeast of Haifa and sixty miles north of Jerusalem. At the appointed time we will dispatch one-third of our forces to overrun the stronghold at Petra.

"The rest of our forces will march on the so-called Eternal City and blast through those infernal walls, destroying all the Jews. And that is where we shall be, joined by our victorious forces from Petra, in full force to surprise the son when he arrives."

Vicki sat, stunned at the shameless way Nicolae was talking about Jesus.

Carpathia's next plan was to use the nuclear weapons stored at Al Hillah. "Needless to say, we do not want or need to destroy the planet. We simply want your soldiers to have more than what they need to wipe out the Jews and destroy the son I have so long opposed. So once I tell you how we will get your military leaders on board, your next assignment will be to get them to Al Hillah, where our Security and Intelligence director,

Mr. Suhail Akbar, will see that they are more than fully equipped."

When the Russian potentate asked how to persuade troops that were discouraged, sick, and injured, Nicole rose. "The time has come to introduce you to three of my most trusted aides. No doubt you have been wondering about the three at the end of the table."

"Wondering why they seem not to have so much as blinked since we sat down," the British potentate said.

Carpathia laughed. "These three are not of this world. They use these shells only when necessary. Indeed, these are spirit beings who have been with me from the beginning. They were among the first who believed in me and saw the lie the father and son were trying to perpetrate in heaven and on earth."

Nicolae and Leon walked to the end of the table.

Lionel sat straight in his chair. "I hope you two have strong stomachs."

"What's going to happen?" Judd said.

"Wait a minute," Vicki said. "Revelation says something about this."

Lionel smiled. "Chapter 16, verses 13 and 14. Good job, Vicki. Dr. Ben-Judah recognized it the first time he saw it too."

"What's that say?" Judd asked.

Lionel stopped the video and pulled up

the verses. " 'And I saw three unclean spirits like frogs coming out of the mouth of the dragon, out of the mouth of the beast, and out of the mouth of the false prophet. For they are spirits of demons, performing signs, which go out to the kings of the earth and of the whole world, to gather them to the battle of that great day of God Almighty.' "

Lionel started the video again.

Nicolae and Leon leaned toward the robotlike creatures and opened their mouths. Out came ugly, slimy, froglike beasts that leaped into the mouths of the three, one from Leon and two from Nicolae.

The three creatures suddenly opened their eyes wide and looked around the room. A camera angle switched, showing their faces, and the three sat back, smiling and nodding to the potentates around the table.

"Please meet Ashtaroth, Baal, and Cankerworm. They are the most convincing and persuasive spirits it has ever been my pleasure to know. I am going to ask now that we, all of us, gather round them and lay hands on them, commissioning them for this momentous task."

"This is so sick," Vicki said.

"Everything Carpathia does mocks God," Judd said.

With the potentates and the others touching the three, Nicolae said, "And now go, you three, to the ends of the earth to gather them to the final conflict in Jerusalem, where we shall once and for all destroy the father and his so-called Messiah. Persuade everyone everywhere that the victory is ours, that we are right, and that together we can destroy the son before he takes over this world. Once he is gone, we will be the undisputed, unopposed leaders of the world.

"I confer upon you the power to perform signs and heal the sick and raise the dead, if need be, to convince the world that victory is ours. And now go in power. . . ."

A huge bolt of lightning flashed on-screen, and the recording went black. When the image returned, Ashtaroth, Baal, and Cankerworm were gone, and Lionel quickly turned the volume down before a noisy peal of thunder erupted.

Nicolae beamed at his audience. Vicki wondered if showing this video would convince some people who Nicolae really was, but she knew most of the world was blind to the truth.

"Farewell, one and all," Nicolae said. "I will see you in six months in the Plain of Megiddo on that great day when victory shall be in sight."

Vicki shuddered as Judd muttered, "I'll be there, Nicky. And I'll see you thrown into hell."

THIRTEEN

Tribulation Christmas

OVER the next several weeks, Judd noticed a flurry of activity in Petra. Nicolae's war plans were in full effect, and his persecution increased. There were more beheadings and more torture of prisoners, and the hunt for Judah-ites continued. News had come of a GC raid in France. A chateau filled with suspected Judah-ites had been discovered, and all the occupants had been beheaded.

Darrion and the others in Illinois wrote that they had moved with Lenore into a hiding place run by a man who had been discovered by Chloe Williams.

"His name is Enoch Dumas," Darrion said over a scratchy phone line. "He was head of a group living in downtown Chicago. That's where Chloe found them and then brought them into the Strong Building."

"Where are they now?" Judd said.

"They split up after they left the Strong Building. Now Enoch and a bunch of his friends are here in Palos Hills. It's a pretty rough group. Lots of former prostitutes and druggies. Sweet people, actually. They know what it means to be forgiven."

Judd explained the persecution they had seen over the past few weeks. "Is it safe there?"

"We're in the basement of an abandoned house. Others are scattered through the neighborhood. There are more than seventy, and Enoch says we'll probably reach a hundred before Jesus comes back."

"You should be careful of newcomers. Never know what the GC will try."

"I know, but what can we do, turn them away? People actually go out and try to find more converts every day. Enoch says we're trying to 'get more drowning people onto the life raft.' "

"Do you have meetings?"

Darrion chuckled. "Yeah, and they're nothing like the Young Trib Force meetings. People come in here, sing, and tell their stories. One man yesterday told how he had kept from taking Carpathia's mark. Not because he was a believer—he was just scared of getting a disease through the tattoo. His name is Adrian, and a GC

Peacekeeper found him one day in a stairwell of some old apartment building. Before the Peacekeeper could react, Adrian hit him over the head with a pipe. Knocked him out cold."

"What did Adrian do then?"

"He went through the Peacekeeper's pockets looking for Nicks or food. You have to understand what it's like on the streets now. There's so much crime, but the GC only seems to be interested in getting people without Carpathia's mark."

"They don't report it on GCNN, but we've heard how bad it's getting."

"Well, guess what Adrian finds in the Peacekeeper's pocket? A pamphlet explaining the gospel. We think the Peacekeeper found it in some church or on a believer. Anyway, this Carpathia follower was actually a missionary because Adrian took the pamphlet, read it, and gave his heart to God."

"Incredible."

"He was so glad to find our group, not just because we have food and can give him protection, but to be near other believers. He didn't know he had the mark of the believer until he got here."

Darrion told him more stories, and Judd asked about Shelly, Conrad, and the others.

"We're doing pretty well. Mark's death shook all of us. I don't know that any of us have gotten over it."

"I know the feeling," Judd said. "But we'll see him again. You know that."

"I can't wait to see my mom and dad and Ryan Daley too."

The mention of Ryan took Judd's breath away.

When he hung up with Darrion he went outside and watched people gather their evening meal. It had been years since Ryan had been with them. He had missed so much of the Tribulation. What would Ryan be like when they saw him again? Would they really be able to recognize him? Would he be the same age as when he died, or would God somehow change his body to be older but still recognizable?

No matter what Ryan looked like—or Mark or Pete or John or the others who had died—Judd knew there was a great reunion ahead.

Vicki stayed busy over the weeks becoming an Internet counselor for young people. After

intense sessions with the elders, Chang
Wong, and Naomi Tiberius, Vicki took her
place beside people of all nationalities who
answered questions from around the world.
She was excited that some of those she coun-
seled were actually airlifted into Petra by Trib
Force pilots.

Vicki knew the suffering and persecution
would end, but as she heard the stories of
hurting and wounded people, she longed for
the return of Jesus even more. She couldn't
wait to see him and hear his voice. She knew
from reading the Scriptures that there were
more prophecies concerning Jesus' second
coming than his first. And this time he
wouldn't come as the lowly, humble servant
but as the mighty, conquering king ready to
defeat his enemies.

Vicki was amazed to see the questions that
came into the Web site. She even received
one from a woman who was clearly not
interested in knowing God but in finding out
when the plague of darkness would be lifted
from New Babylon.

"How could she believe that we have
answers from the Bible but not believe the
truth about God?" Vicki asked Judd as they
ate one night.

"She's blind," Judd said. "These people

know there's something to the claims of the Bible, but they follow Carpathia anyway. Those troops know how many soldiers God wiped out, but they still follow orders."

There was a slight knock on the door, and Judd opened it to find Sam Goldberg. Sam sat and had some wafers and quail. Judd and Vicki had been secretly talking with him about a possible trip to Israel before the start of the last great battle.

"Have you found anyone yet?" Judd asked.

"My friend Lev Taubman is from Jerusalem," Sam said quietly. "He wants to go back there badly, but his mother won't hear of it."

"Does he know any hiding places, any members of the resistance?" Vicki said.

"There is a man my father was acquainted with," Sam said. "Very old. His name is Shivte. Lev says he and his sons would never take the mark of Carpathia, but they are not believers either."

"You think they're still in Jerusalem?"

"Lev is sure of it because he received a message from another friend saying Shivte's wife has become a true believer. And with what I hear about . . ." Sam stopped and stared at them.

"What is it?" Vicki said.

"I'm not sure I should tell you what I heard about Dr. Ben-Judah."

"What, that he's teaching an elite group of Captain Steele's military people?" Judd said. "We know that."

"Did you know he has officially turned over his administrative and teaching duties for Petra to Dr. Rosenzweig?" Sam said.

"*What?*" Judd and Vicki said in unison.

"I can't tell you where I heard this, but I believe Tsion wants to be part of the fighting force in Jerusalem. He's been training to use a weapon."

"I don't believe it," Vicki said.

Sam leaned closer. "This is what I have heard. Tsion believes the Bible teaches that a third of the remaining Jews will turn to Messiah before the end. That means that many will still need to be reached, and Tsion thinks if he can get to Jerusalem, he can reach them."

Judd scratched the stubble of his beard. "It makes sense, I guess."

"Now I don't feel so bad wanting to get to Jerusalem to see Jesus return," Vicki said.

"Where does Tsion get that more Jews will come to Messiah?" Judd said.

"It's in Zechariah 13. Verses 8 and 9."

Vicki grabbed a Bible, flipped toward the end of the Old Testament. " '"And it shall come to pass in all the land," says the Lord,

"That two-thirds in it shall be cut off and die, but one-third shall be left in it: I will bring the one-third through the fire, will refine them as silver is refined, and test them as gold is tested. They will call on My name, and I will answer them. I will say, 'This is My people'; and each one will say, 'The Lord is my God.' " "

As Vicki read the verses, something stirred inside her. If there were more Jews who would accept Jesus as Messiah, they had to be hiding. If she and Judd could help find them and prepare them in some way for the message . . . She looked at Judd and could tell he was thinking the same thing.

Lionel ate breakfast with Zeke Zuckermandel at least once a week and caught up on the latest with the Tribulation Force. Zeke was fun to talk with, and the two relived their days in Illinois and Wisconsin.

"You about ready to come out of that place with all the fancy computers and get yourself dirty?" Zeke said.

"What do you mean?" Lionel said.

"Just that I'm getting a band of people together to help out during the war."

"Tell me about it."

Zeke leaned forward and drew a finger through the sand. "This here is Petra with all the rocks and stuff. Here's the desert in front of us and around us, and all the way over here is Israel. Now, most people are mixed up about the Battle of Armageddon."

"How so?"

"This comes straight from Tsion himself. This valley of Armageddon is really just the staging area for Carpathia's armies. You know, where they set up, eat, prepare, that kinda thing. The actual wars are gonna take place here at Petra—" he pointed to the circle in the sand—"although you have to believe God won't let the armies have a victory here, and over here in Jerusalem. Tsion says people should call this 'the War of the Great Day of God the Almighty.' But I can see how sayin' it's Armageddon's just plain easier."

"I'm still confused about what's going to happen when," Lionel said.

"Tsion says there are going to be something like eight things happening after the Euphrates River goes dry."

"What's so important about that?"

"Well, you ever see an army try to get across a river that's running? When it dries up, the kings and armies east of here will have a clear shot at us. They can come into this valley—it's called Megiddo—and be ready for the trap."

"What trap?"

"Well, Tsion says this is exactly what God wants. It'll look like there's no way anyone can stand up to the strength of all those tanks and missiles and troops, but God's gonna zap 'em."

"What else happens?"

"Once the river goes dry and the armies get together, Babylon will be destroyed. God's gonna do that real quick, and then comes the fall of Jerusalem. I'm kinda hazy about how that happens, but finally Jesus will appear on a white horse with a big army of his own. He'll be mad at old Nicolae, and there's gonna be a lot of blood, you can bet on that. There's gonna be a battle close to here, though Petra will be safe. And then Jesus will show up at the Mount of Olives."

"Wish I could be there," Lionel said.

"You and me both. But there's plenty to do here. As a matter of fact, I'm looking for some volunteers."

"Is this the getting myself dirty part?"

Zeke smiled. "You got it. I need people to go out and pick up weapons, uniforms, ammo—just about anything you think we could use."

"Sounds dangerous."

"Could be. But my guess is the GC won't have any power over believers who are living here in Petra. God's gonna protect us."

"You don't know that for sure."

"Right. Not 100 percent, but I'm willing to chance it. How about you?"

Judd went to the airstrip in late December and met with Mac McCullum. Mac, Abdullah Smith, and Ree Woo had become the main pilots for the Tribulation Force, and they had recruited other pilots to help fly believers to Petra from all over the world. Mac had tons of stories of miraculous things God had done to keep believers safe, but this was a short meeting.

"Found what you were looking for in Morocco," Mac said, handing Judd a small box. "Hope the little lady enjoys it."

Judd thanked him and raced back to their empty house. Vicki had finished her work at the tech center for the day and was spending some time with little Kenny.

Judd quickly went behind their house to a rock outcropping where he had seen a small bush. After he dug the plant up by its roots and put it in a pot, he placed it on the nightstand. He cut strips of cloth and draped them around the bush, then set the wrapped box on one of the sturdy branches.

He watched for Vicki for nearly an hour. When he saw her coming, he hid in a corner of the room and waited.

"Judd?" Vicki called as she came close. "Mr. Thompson? Are you home?" She walked inside and saw the bush. "What in the world?"

Judd started humming a Christmas tune.

Vicki caught her breath. "What's going on?"

"Just because we're in the middle of the Tribulation doesn't mean we can't celebrate, right?"

"It's December 25th! I forgot all about it."

Judd pointed at the tiny, crudely wrapped present in the bush. Vicki just stared at it, her mouth open. Judd handed her the box and she opened it slowly, the fading sunlight twinkling off the stone in the middle of the ring.

She couldn't say anything for a moment. Then, "It must have cost a fortune."

"I didn't have a chance to get you a ring when we were married. Mac found a jeweler on one of his flights, and he got a bargain. The jeweler thinks it'll last at least a thousand years."

Vicki smiled. "I hope we get to find out if he's right."

FOURTEEN

To Jerusalem

LIONEL awoke from another nightmare and wiped sweat from his forehead. On some nights he dreamed about dogs chasing him, barking and biting at something trapped under a rock. Other nights Lionel dreamed of a dragon chasing his friends toward a cliff. At the edge of the cliff was a huge army.

This time he had dreamed of Judd and Vicki being caught by the Global Community. He knew it had something to do with their leaving the day before. Lionel had promised he wouldn't say anything to Chang or anyone else about their secret departure. Judd had been sure Captain Steele would have stopped them.

When Judd had discovered that Westin Jakes, Z-Van's former pilot, had caught an airlift out of the desert near New Babylon and was again flying for the Tribulation Force, Judd had asked a favor. Lionel had seen them off to the airstrip and waved good-bye, not knowing if he would ever see his friends again.

Lionel got a glass of water and looked out the screenless window at the lightening sky. The sight of Petra in the morning never ceased to move him. The red-rocked city seemed to glow at both sunup and sundown.

Lionel quietly went to the tech center. He kept in contact with his friends in Illinois and e-mailed a new friend in New Babylon, of all places. Through Tsion's Web site Lionel had met a young German woman named Steffi. She was with a group that had stayed in the still-darkened city. She reported that nothing much had changed. People were still screaming and chewing their tongues, and the believers were able to move through the city undetected.

Lionel, is there a way I could call your phone and talk about our airlift out of here? Steffi wrote. *I know that our main connection is through Otto Weser and you probably don't have much to do with that, but it would calm my nerves if I could talk.*

Lionel wrote back, giving Steffi a number and a time. As soon as he sent the message, another message popped up.

Lionel,

We finally made it to Shivte's house a little after four this morning and wanted you to know we're okay. We're supposed to meet with some of the resistance fighters later.

The flight out of Petra was a little scary, but Westin found the landing strip. Then we hooked up with one of Shivte's sons and made the drive into Jerusalem without being spotted by the GC.

Westin told us the most amazing story about getting out of New Babylon. He and his friends found an abandoned terrorist training camp and holed up there for a while. Westin got a flight out through the Trib Force, but Judd's friend Zvi and some of the others decided to go back into New Babylon.

Thanks for praying for us, and don't worry. We're not planning to do any fighting, just trying to reach out to Jewish people who haven't accepted their Messiah.

Take care and we'll call you soon.

Love,
Vicki

Lionel shook his head. Most people would try to stay as safe as they could during the final battle. But after all Judd and Vicki had been through, they still wanted to reach people with the message of God's love and forgiveness.

Judd shook hands with Shivte in the dimly lit home and introduced Vicki. The elderly man shuffled to the kitchen table of their small home. He and his sons were stocky men and soft-spoken. None of them had the mark of the believer.

Shivte asked one of his sons to get his wife, then motioned for Judd and Vicki to sit. "You should know that it was my wife who arranged this," he said. "And I only agreed to help you come here on the condition that you would not try to get us to change our beliefs."

Judd pursed his lips. "As I wrote from Petra, we don't want to get in the way. We just want to support the resistance effort in any way we can."

"My son will show you to one of the underground hideouts," Shivte said. "There are military people there who can show you what is needed."

Shivte offered them some meager rations, which Judd and Vicki politely refused. "We brought some supplies with us," Judd said. "It would please us if you would take them."

Shivte nodded. "We're grateful."

Shivte's wife came through the doorway, smiling. She was a large woman with heavy lines in her face, and Judd thought she looked a lot like his grandmother. When she spotted the mark of the believer on their foreheads, Judd thought she would weep. She hugged them both and thanked them for bringing food.

"How I would have liked to have experienced Petra, if only for a few days," the woman said. "I can only imagine the teaching and fellowship you enjoyed there." She glanced at her husband. "But there are more pressing matters here. You can see that I have not yet convinced the most important people in my life of the truth."

Shivte stood and waved a hand at her. "I'm not staying to hear this."

"Will you go get the people now?" she said.

Shivte nodded and left the house.

"Who is he going to get?" Judd said.

"You'll see," Shivte's wife said.

"How did you become a believer?" Vicki said.

"I didn't plan on it," she said. "My husband and sons said they would not take

Carpathia's mark, but we had to have food. So I volunteered to take it so I could buy and sell. The idea of worshiping that statue . . . well, I couldn't imagine it, but we had to survive."

"How close did you come to taking it?" Judd said.

"I was at the Temple Mount, in line. I thought it was the only way to save my family. But then I saw a disturbance and slipped out of line. A man of God was shot—his name was Micah—but the bullets didn't kill him. After that, I had to know more about this message. I have a young friend, the one who wrote your friend Sam, and he helped me find Tsion Ben-Judah's Web site."

"And your husband and sons?" Vicki said.

"We have agreed not to talk about it. They are devout Jews, and they will resist Carpathia to the end, but they are not ready for Messiah. How I pray for them every day that somehow the message will get through."

Footsteps sounded on the street outside. Shivte's wife stood and motioned for Judd and Vicki to follow her to the door. "I was talking with a friend about you two and where you would stay. We have very little room here. One conversation led to another, and finally I discovered that—"

The door opened and a man and a woman

walked through. In the dim light, Judd couldn't see their faces. When they moved closer, his mouth dropped open. "I don't believe it!"

The two hugged Judd tightly and wept. Judd turned to Vicki. "Remember Nada and Kasim? These are their parents, Jamal and Lina Ameer."

Lina reached out and hugged Vicki. "So this is the person Judd was in love with. You're very beautiful, my dear."

Vicki blushed. "I'm very sorry about your son and daughter. Our group back in the States prayed for you almost every day."

"We appreciate that more than you can know," Jamal said.

"We couldn't believe it when we heard you were coming," Lina said. "We'd love to hear what God has done since we last talked. How is Lionel?"

They sat at the table and Judd explained about Lionel's injury and how they had gotten back to the States. The two were saddened to hear about Lionel's arm but were glad he was safe in Petra.

Judd asked if they knew anything about the rebel fighters, and Jamal pulled out a crude map. "There are underground tunnels through here. Many people have hidden in them since the GC took over. We have weapons and ammunition, even some computers to help us track the movement of the GC One World Unity Army's troops. We can go through there as we head to our apartment. You will stay with us."

Shivte closed the door quietly and put a finger to his lips. "We must hide. The GC are going house to house down the street."

Judd and Vicki followed the others to a hiding place under the stairs.

"Does this happen often?" Vicki whispered to Jamal.

"All the time," Jamal said.

Lionel took Steffi's call and listened to her story. It was much like others he had heard from people who had already come out of New Babylon. Her father wanted to be in Carpathia's city to fulfill prophecy, but things had become so horrible there with the plague of darkness that Steffi couldn't imagine staying any longer.

"Fortunately, I think you'll be out of there pretty soon," Lionel said. "The seven-year anniversary of Carpathia's peace treaty with Israel is coming up in only a few days."

"I've longed for the coming of Jesus," Steffi

said. "I've been afraid the plague of darkness will lift and the GC will catch my father."

"Does he spend a lot of time in GC areas?" Lionel said.

"The palace, the prison—wherever he thinks he can find information or a possible person who doesn't have the mark of the believer. I've told him he should be more careful. . . ."

Lionel pulled the phone away from his ear. Something odd was happening in Chang Wong's area. "Hang on a second, Steffi."

Chang was standing and pointing to his computer screen. "It's happened!"

Others came running.

"What's happened?" Lionel said, but Chang didn't hear him.

"What's going on?" Steffi said.

"It might be something with the Euphrates River," Lionel said. "Chang's been watching sensors planted there by the GC—"

Before Lionel could finish his sentence, Chang turned to Naomi Tiberius and said, "There was water in the Euphrates a minute ago, and now it is dry as a bone. You can bet tomorrow it will be on the news—someone standing in the dry, cracking riverbed, show-ing that you can walk across without fear of mud or quicksand."

"That is amazing," Naomi said. "I mean, I knew it was coming, but isn't it just like God to do it all at once? And isn't that a 1,500-mile river?"

"It used to be."

Lionel explained what he had heard to Steffi, and she gave an excited shout. "This means the Lord's return is that much closer."

Lionel finished the conversation and joined Chang and the others.

Later a Trib Force scout plane reported vast weapons and troop movement toward the dried-up river. Lionel figured Carpathia had been reading the Bible but was too stupid to understand how the book ended.

Vicki was excited about Jamal and Lina's spacious apartment. The two offered to give Judd and Vicki their bedroom, but instead they put down sleeping bags from Petra in the living room.

The next few weeks Judd and Vicki spent time getting to know the complex series of passageways underneath Jerusalem. It would be their job to supply ammunition to the rebel forces seeking to keep the GC away.

"We respect your wish to not be involved in the actual fighting," Jamal said, "but your job will be just as critical to defending Jerusalem."

After dinner one evening, Lina showed Vicki pictures of their family and pointed out Kasim and Nada. "I miss them both very much, but it won't be long before we're together again."

"It might be sooner than we think," Jamal said. "Judd just showed me an intercepted message from a top Global Community officer."

"What did it say?" Vicki said.

"Basically, it warned all Peacekeepers and Morale Monitors throughout the world to prepare for a new assignment in the Middle East. We think it will only be a few days before hundreds of thousands join the GC One World Unity Army."

"Which means people without Carpathia's mark will be able to come out of hiding," Vicki said.

"As long as they're careful," Judd said. "Citizens can still kill people without the mark and get a reward. But it looks like the end is close."

Lionel was talking with Sam Goldberg when he noticed Rayford Steele running toward the helipad. Lionel and Sam walked to a rock outcropping as droves of people headed for a clearing.

"What's going on?" Lionel said.

"Maybe it's the evacuation of New Babylon," Sam said. "I heard that pilots from here will fly the rescue mission as soon as word comes that believers are to move out."

"They'd need something bigger than a helicopter, don't you think?" Lionel said.

Many people near the chopper wept. Sam climbed down and ran to the edge of the crowd, then returned. "They're saying goodbye to Dr. Ben-Judah. He's going to Jerusalem."

A few moments later, Tsion and Buck Williams moved through the crowd. Tsion pulled what looked to Lionel like a handkerchief from his pocket and waved it as Buck climbed aboard the chopper.

"People! People!" Tsion shouted. "I am overwhelmed at your kindness. Pray for me, won't you, that I will be privileged to usher many more into the kingdom. We are just days away now from the battle, and you know what that means. Be waiting and watching. Be ready for the Glorious Appearing! If I am not back before then, we will be reunited soon thereafter.

"You will be in my thoughts and prayers,

and I know I go with yours. Thank you again! You are in good hands with Chaim Rosenzweig, and so I bid you farewell!" Tsion kept waving at the people as the helicopter lifted off.

"Wish we could be going to Jerusalem," Sam said.

"You're part of Zeke's brigade," Lionel said. "There'll be plenty of action here."

Lionel sprinted toward the tech center. He couldn't wait to tell Judd and Vicki that Tsion was heading their way.

FIFTEEN

Rumbling Earth

JUDD's head spun with Lionel's news of
Tsion's departure from Petra. Then Chang
Wong reported that hundreds of thousands
of troops would arrive in the valley of
Megiddo the following day. Everything was
happening so fast.

"That's going to be a nightmare to feed
and equip all those soldiers," Vicki said.

"The Global Community's been preparing
for this a long time," Jamal said. "They'll find
a way to mass their troops."

With the help of others, Judd and Vicki
placed ammunition boxes in strategic places
throughout the tunnels. When the fighting
began in Jerusalem, they would be able to get
ammo to rebels within minutes.

"They keep talking about a guerilla war,"
Vicki said. "What's that mean?"

"Lots of little wars throughout the city," Judd said. "Basically the rebels know they have no chance of beating this army head-on, so they're going to spread out and try to make it as difficult as possible for the GC."

Rebel leaders barked orders, and young men and women prepared for battle. Teams of workers went into the street to set up barricades.

"Chopper's landing at the Temple Mount," one man yelled as he ran through the tunnel to get more Uzis and grenades.

Judd grabbed the man by the arm. "Is it a GC chopper?"

"Didn't look like it, but I didn't stay long. There's an angry mob out there."

"You think that's Tsion?" Vicki said.

"Has to be," Judd said.

It took Judd a few minutes to get his bearings once he and Vicki had climbed out of their hiding place. Making sure there were no Global Community forces nearby, they headed for the Temple Mount.

Judd was surprised to see old men praying at the Wailing Wall, something they hadn't been allowed to do for a long time. "I haven't seen so many unmarked people since Masada."

"These people must have been in hiding for years," Vicki said. "But you can tell they're scared."

"They're scared, but you have to understand. This is their city. They'll do anything
to defend it."

"Even if it's going to fall?" Vicki said. "You
know Tsion believes it will."

Judd took Vicki's hand, and they ran to the
place where Judd had seen the two witnesses,
Eli and Moishe. He wished they would come
back now and preach.

Suddenly there was a commotion when a
man with a gun at his side pushed his way
through the crowd at the Wailing Wall. He
wore loose-fitting canvas-type clothing and a
jacket. On his head was the traditional cover-
ing of the Jews, a yarmulke. "Men of Israel,
hear me!" he bellowed. "I am one of you! I
come with news!"

"It's Tsion!" Judd whispered. "Come on!"

They pushed their way to the edge of the
gathering, then climbed higher for a better
look. Men yelled at Tsion, but Judd couldn't
tell what they were saying.

Finally, Tsion said, "What you need is
Messiah!"

Some cheered, many laughed, and even
more grumbled. Judd caught sight of Buck
Williams.

"Many of you know me! I am Tsion Ben-
Judah. I became persona non grata when I

broadcast my findings after being commissioned to study the prophecies concerning Messiah. My family was slaughtered. I was exiled. A bounty remains on my head."

"Then why are you here, man? Do you not know the Global Community devils are coming back?"

"I do not fear them, because Messiah is coming too! Do not scoff! Do not turn your backs on me! Listen to our own Scriptures. What do you think this means?" He read Zechariah 12:8-10: " 'In that day the Lord will defend the inhabitants of Jerusalem; the one who is feeble among them in that day shall be like David, and the house of David shall be like God, like the Angel of the Lord before them. It shall be in that day that I will seek to destroy all the nations that come against Jerusalem.

" 'And I will pour on the house of David and on the inhabitants of Jerusalem the Spirit of grace and supplication; then they will look on Me whom they pierced. Yes, they will mourn for Him as one mourns for his only son, and grieve for Him as one grieves for a firstborn.' "

Judd felt tears coming to his eyes and glanced at Vicki. She was overwhelmed with emotion too.

"You tell us what it means!" someone yelled.

"God is saying he will make the weakest among us as strong as David," Tsion said. "And he will destroy the nations that come against us. My dear friends, that is all the other nations of the earth!"

"We know. Carpathia has made it no secret!"

"But God says we will finally look upon 'Me whom they pierced,' and that we will mourn him as we would mourn the loss of a firstborn son. Messiah was pierced! And God refers to the pierced one as 'Me'! Messiah is also God.

"Beloved, my exhaustive study of the hundreds of prophecies concerning Messiah brought me to the only logical conclusion. Messiah was born of a virgin in Bethlehem. He lived without sin. He was falsely accused. He was slain without cause. He died and was buried and was raised after three days. Those prophecies alone point to Jesus of Nazareth as Messiah. He is the one who is coming to fight for Israel. He will avenge all the wrongs that have been perpetrated upon us over the centuries.

"The time is short. The day of salvation is here. You may not have time to study this for yourselves. Messiah is God's promise to us.

Jesus is the fulfillment of that promise. He is coming. Let him find you ready!"

People shouted at Tsion, clearly offended. Some walked away, but others seemed to want to hear more. Even with all the noise and confusion the crowd grew, and Judd was worried Peacekeepers or Morale Monitors might show up.

Tsion kept talking, quoting Scripture, and explaining it. He spoke of the armies gathering to destroy them, but he urged the people not to be afraid of them but to be ready for the Messiah.

"If you want to know how to be prepared for him," Tsion yelled, "gather here to my left and my associate will tell you. Please! Come now! Don't delay! Now is the accepted time. Today is the day of salvation."

Vicki looked at Judd. "Does he mean Buck?"

Judd nodded in amazement. Buck wasn't Jewish and was a reporter, not a preacher.

But to Judd's astonishment, Buck began speaking after a short pause. "When Jewish people such as yourselves come to see that Jesus is your long-sought Messiah, you are not converting from one religion to another, no matter what anyone tells you. You have found your Messiah, that is all. Some would say you have been completed, fulfilled. Everything you have studied and been told all your life is the foundation for your acceptance of Messiah and what he has done for you."

Tsion bowed his head in prayer as Buck told the men how to accept God's gift of salvation through Jesus. "He comes not only to avenge Jerusalem but to save your soul, to forgive your sins, to grant you eternal life with God."

Lionel stared at the computer screen, now split into two sections. On one side he watched troop movement into the valley outside Jerusalem. On the other he monitored GCNN's coverage of the pending battle. For the last several days, reporters had talked about the Euphrates River drying up.

Now they focused on Nicolae Carpathia riding a huge, black horse. The man held a long sword and grinned from ear to ear. "We have the absolute latest in technology and power at our fingertips," Carpathia shouted. "My months of strategy are over, and we have a foolproof plan. That frees me to encourage the troops, to be flown to the battle sites, to mount up, to be a visual reminder that victory is in sight and will soon be in hand.

"It will not be long, my brothers and sisters

in the Global Community, until we shall reign victorious. I shall return to rebuild my throne as conquering king. The world shall finally be as one! It is not too early to rejoice!"

Vicki couldn't believe that she was seeing prophecy fulfilled before her eyes. As Buck prayed with people pressing toward him, Tsion Ben-Judah told others the truth about Jesus, and more Jews streamed in to hear the message. The people who had rejected Jesus for so long now believed he was their Messiah.

Crowds surged around Tsion and Buck. Soon thousands wept aloud and fell to their knees, asking God's forgiveness.

Tsion continued his message, telling the throng that the armies gathered nearby would face another terror from God, a mighty earthquake. He said hail weighing as much as one hundred pounds would fall to the earth, crushing people.

"Do you know what will happen here, right here in Jerusalem?" Tsion said. "It will be the only city in the world spared the devastating destruction of the greatest earthquake ever known to man. The Bible says, 'Now the great city'—that's Jerusalem—'was divided into three parts, and the cities of the nations fell.'

"That, my brothers, is good news. Jerusalem will be made more beautiful, more efficient. It will be prepared for its role as the new capital in Messiah's thousand-year kingdom."

Lionel wrote a quick report to the rest of the Young Trib Force and hoped they would see it. There was so much activity in the tech center that Lionel had to put on headphones to hear the latest from GCNN. With a click of a button, he viewed a camera mounted at the top of Petra. Below the edges of the rock walls, platoons of soldiers prepared their weapons. He clicked on GCNN, which showed an aerial picture of Nicolae's army, and shook his head. *A few thousand soldiers against that?*

His phone rang and he was surprised to hear Steffi on the other end. Her voice trembled with fear. "We've been watching the coverage about the battle. I'm afraid we've waited too long to get out of here."

Lionel explained what he knew about the rescue effort and told Steffi that Mac McCullum would fly there. "Where are you now?"

"Outside of our hiding place on the—" Steffi stopped, then gasped.

"What is it?" Lionel said.

"Something so bright that the darkness is gone!" she said. "It's big. Very big."

Before Lionel could ask another question, a piercing male voice sounded through the phone. " 'Babylon the great is fallen, is fallen, and has become a dwelling place of demons, a prison for every foul spirit, and a cage for every unclean and hated bird! . . .' "

Lionel raised a fist in the air. "Steffi, that's the angel! I'll go tell Mr. McCullum. He'll come get you!"

But before Lionel could hang up, another voice said, " 'Come out of her, my people, lest you share in her sins, and lest you receive of her plagues. For her sins have reached to heaven, and God has remembered her iniquities.' "

As soon as Lionel hung up, he raced to find Mac. He finally found him at his airplane, firing up the engines.

Mac had heard the report from someone else and was on his way to New Babylon. "Got room for one more, if you'd like to come along," he said.

Lionel climbed on board while Mac called for another plane to help evacuate believers. "With these two planes, I figure we should be able to bring up to two hundred people out of there. I hope that's enough."

They landed near the palace and Lionel gasped. People who had been living in darkness wandered about the runway, limping and staggering, not knowing what to do.

As soon as the plane stopped, Lionel helped Mac get the stairs down. More than 150 believers cheered outside. The other plane landed and took half of the believers who carried their belongings in sacks and boxes. Loading took only a few minutes, and they were ready to go.

Lionel looked at the faces of people as they boarded, wondering which one was Judd's friend Zvi. Lionel saw a blonde young lady with an older woman and approached her. "Steffi?"

"Lionel?"

The two hugged, and Steffi introduced Lionel to her mom.

"No time for chitchat," Mac said. "Let's get out of here."

Soon the planes raced down the runways. Before the wheels of Mac's plane were off the ground, Lionel noticed a volley of missiles being launched from just outside the city. As the planes rose higher, black smoke engulfed the once gleaming city. Mac circled as missile after missile hit the heart of New Babylon, destroying the entire city in less than one hour.

As darkness fell, Judd and Vicki broke away from Tsion's preaching and scurried underground. The news of Babylon's fall had reached them through Tsion's Web site. Believers in the underground passage were excited about Judd and Vicki's news that thousands of Jews were turning to Christ, but unbelievers scoffed.

"If Babylon has fallen," Vicki said, "that means there are only two prophetic events left."

"The seventh Bowl Judgment and the Glorious Appearing," Judd said.

Vicki nodded. "And if that's true, should we stay here and feed ammo to a losing cause or try to convince as many people as possible that they need Christ?"

"I don't want to let the resistance down, but a lot of people are hungry for the message. After all, once these people die, we won't have another chance."

Judd thought about Vicki's idea while he found something for them to eat. A supply area had pita bread and peanut butter, but that was about it.

When he returned, Vicki was talking with a female Jewish rebel without Carpathia's mark. *Reaching more people is what this is all about,* Judd thought.

When she finished with the woman—who did not pray—Vicki seemed even more animated. "There are so many like her all around us. If we can get to them tonight before—"

A noise interrupted her. Several rebel leaders rushed into the tunnel. Walls vibrated, and lights clinked against ancient stone walls. At first Judd thought it was an earthquake. Then he realized the truth.

It was the rumble of Carpathia's army.

ABOUT THE AUTHORS

Jerry B. Jenkins (www.jerryjenkins.com) is the writer of the Left Behind series. He owns the Jerry B. Jenkins Christian Writers Guild, an organization dedicated to mentoring aspiring authors. Former vice president for publishing for the Moody Bible Institute of Chicago, he also served many years as editor of *Moody* magazine and is now Moody's writer-at-large.

His writing has appeared in publications as varied as *Reader's Digest, Parade, Guideposts*, in-flight magazines, and dozens of other periodicals. Jenkins's biographies include books with Billy Graham, Hank Aaron, Bill Gaither, Luis Palau, Walter Payton, Orel Hershiser, and Nolan Ryan, among many others. His books appear regularly on the *New York Times, USA Today, Wall Street Journal*, and *Publishers Weekly* best-seller lists.

Jerry is also the writer of the nationally syndicated sports story comic strip *Gil Thorp*, distributed to newspapers across the United States by Tribune Media Services.

Jerry and his wife, Dianna, live in Colorado and have three grown sons.

Dr. Tim LaHaye (www.timlahaye.com), who conceived the idea of fictionalizing an account of the Rapture and the Tribulation, is a noted author, minister, and nationally recognized speaker on Bible prophecy. He is the founder of both Tim LaHaye Ministries and The PreTrib Research Center. He also recently cofounded the Tim LaHaye School of Prophecy at Liberty University. Presently Dr. LaHaye speaks at many of the major Bible prophecy conferences in the U.S. and Canada, where his current prophecy books are very popular.

Dr. LaHaye holds a doctor of ministry degree from Western Theological Seminary and a doctor of literature degree from Liberty University. For twenty-five years he pastored one of the nation's outstanding churches in San Diego, which grew to three locations. It was during that time that he founded two accredited Christian high schools, a Christian school system of ten schools, and Christian Heritage College.

Dr. LaHaye has written over forty books that have been published in more than thirty languages. He has written books on a wide variety of subjects, such as family life, temperaments, and Bible prophecy. His current fiction works, the Left Behind series, written with Jerry B. Jenkins, continue to appear on the bestseller lists of the Christian Booksellers Association, *Publishers Weekly*, *Wall Street Journal*, *USA Today*, and the *New York Times*.

He is the father of four grown children and grandfather of nine. Snow skiing, waterskiing, motorcycling, golfing, vacationing with family, and jogging are among his leisure activities.

Hooked on the exciting
Left Behind: The Kids series?
Then you'll love the dramatic audios!

Listen as the characters come to life in this theatrical
audio that makes the saga of those left behind
even more exciting.

High-tech sound effects, original music,
and professional actors will have you
on the edge of your seat.

Experience the heart-stopping action and
suspense of the end times for yourself!

Five exciting volumes available on CD or cassette.

The Future Is Clear

Check out the exciting Left Behind: The Kids series